THE
WATCHER

ALSO BY CAROLINE ERIKSSON

The Missing

THE
WATCHER

CAROLINE ERIKSSON

TRANSLATED BY TARA F. CHACE

Previously published as *Hon som vakar* by Forum in 2017 in Sweden. Translated from Swedish by Tara F. Chace. First published in English by AmazonCrossing in 2018.

Published by AmazonCrossing, Seattle

www.apub.com

Amazon, the Amazon logo, and AmazonCrossing are trademarks of Amazon.com, Inc., or its affiliates.

ISBN-13: 9781503905405
ISBN-10: 1503905403

Cover design by David Drummond

Printed in the United States of America

To Mom and Dad
For what was
For what is
For all we have left

PROLOGUE

THE HUSBAND

So this is how it's going to end?

I'm teetering on the edge. I turn around and our eyes meet, hers the same ones that once looked into mine at the altar in that picturesque little village church. They were filled with happiness and emotion then, but now they're black with the hatred of revenge. And I see decisiveness in her face, a purposefulness that hasn't been there for a long time. Only now does it occur to me that what's about to happen is not a coincidence. My wife has been waiting for an opportunity like this. She wants to see me dead.

This whole time I've been worried about her . . . Suddenly I realize that I should have been afraid for myself.

People say that in your final moments you see your life pass before your eyes, from beginning to end. How would anyone even know something like that? I don't experience it. No cavalcade of birthdays and celebrations, flickers of failures and successes, or the faces that I held most dear. I see only one thing in front of me, and, oddly enough, it's that church where we once promised to love each other forever, for better or for worse. I remember everything, every single detail of our wedding day, just as clearly as if it were yesterday—our fingers intertwined as we slowly walked down the aisle, the smiling faces in the pews, the rustling of fancy clothes, the scent of freshly picked summer flowers, our vows that we'd written ourselves, the sun shining through the stained-glass windows, the pastor's blessing.

And now? Is this—this church where we swore to love each other until death do us part—where she'll bury me, or rather, what's left of me?

The chasm before me is deep and unforgiving. It contains no uncertainty, no mercy. Everything is happening so quickly, and yet this moment stretches out for an eternity. She comes closer, right up beside me. She raises one hand, then the other. Soon I'll fall. Soon I'll be dashed to pieces. Soon it will be over.

Three, two, one.

Now.

1

Just before four o'clock, I get up and throw on my bathrobe. I'd stopped counting the hours and minutes I lay awake at night ages ago. It's not even a month since the separation, and I haven't gotten used to sleeping alone yet. I can't imagine I ever will. On a purely physical level, I miss Peter. Even the first night we slept together, it was like our bodies had found their way home, as if they had slipped into each other's nooks and filled each other's crannies. I'd slept in different people's arms before, but I'd never experienced anything like this. Peter felt it, too. "We're like a puzzle," he whispered into my ear, "with only two pieces."

The staircase leading downstairs is shrouded in nighttime darkness. The steps are steep and narrow, easy to slip on if you're not careful. I close my eyes and lean forward, feel my body's center of gravity being sucked farther and farther over the landing. If I started walking with my eyes closed, if I let fate have its way, maybe I would make it all the way down, descending calmly and steadily. I lean even farther forward. I don't actually even need to try taking a step, don't need to antici- pate fate. There's another alternative: to throw myself headlong into the darkness. I can make sure to land on my head, allowing my neck to break under the weight of my body. One life extinguished in the night, one drop in the vast cosmos.

It's not the first time this idea occurs to me. But just as before, the thought leads to my sister. To the realization that she would be the one to find me; she would be the one forced to deal with all the practical matters. Of the family that once existed, only the two of us remain. *I can't do that to her.* My hand reaches for the light switch. An instant later, the light pours over the stairs and I descend, step by step.

I walk through the empty town house in a little development built around a landscaped communal yard. This place is meant to play the part of my home now, although it actually belongs to someone else. I am a shadowy figure in this existence, passing through on my way elsewhere. The rent has been paid in advance for three months. I have no idea where I'll go after this. Maybe that should worry me, but I feel nothing.

In the kitchen I pour myself a glass of water and drink it while leaning back against the sink. The unit across the yard is dark. I see no lights on in any of the windows. The people who live there are probably asleep, like all normal, sensible people at this hour. Safe and undisturbed, with the ones they love most in the next room or in bed beside them. My borrowed twin bed awaits in the bedroom upstairs. The bed will be cool when I return. No one is keeping it warm under the covers. There will be no legs to press the freezing soles of my feet against, no one whose neck and back I can nestle up against and shape my body to.

A puzzle with only two pieces. I used that phrase once in a story. When the manuscript came back, I saw that the editor had drawn two red lines through those specific words and written "Kind of cliché" in the margin. She couldn't have known how special those words were to me. She was just doing her job, and I accepted the edit. But maybe I should have stood my ground. Those words meant something to me. A publisher's opinions are suggestions—usually prudent ones—but ultimately the author has final say over her own text. I'll remember that next time. *In my next manuscript, I'll . . .* The thought flows into nothingness. I empty my glass and shake my head. *Next time, next manuscript, who am I kidding?* I haven't written a line in almost two years.

I continue moving through the house, following the same pattern I usually do during these nightly ambles, and soon wind up in the living room. It's not a big room, and yet it contains most of what I brought when I left the home Peter and I shared. The moving boxes stacked along the walls are filled with things I haven't bothered to unpack—meaningless objects, relics from a time that will never return. There's only one thing here that means anything to me.

My steps slow, and I move over to the bookshelf. I reach out my arm and carefully run my hand over the densely packed rows of book spines. There are so many stories between their covers, the fates of so many lives. They relate the joy and pain of being human, the cruelties to which we subject each other. There are certain common themes in all stories, just as in all human life, and I know that I'm not alone in my adventures and experiences, although it feels like it. *Oh, Mama, if you could see me now.*

My hands select by themselves, moving as if they belong to someone else, as if they have a life of their own. One book at a time is pulled out and assigned a new place—sometimes on the same shelf, but more often than not somewhere else. At first it happens slowly, almost randomly, then with more and more focus. Book after book is repositioned, ending up higher, lower, closer to the middle or to the edge. Tonight I'm sorting by title, but my actual criteria are unimportant. What matters is having something to do to keep the turbulence below the surface at bay.

Some of the shelves are crowded, so I hold the books awaiting reshelving in my lap and continue working with one hand. Empty spaces appear and are filled again. One context is undone and a new totality gradually emerges. But it doesn't help, of course. Nothing helps. When I finally stand in front of the bookshelf and survey the results, everything is different. And yet it's exactly the same. I slowly back out of the room.

The next time I become aware of anything, it's grown so cold. My legs feel cold on the inside. Then something extremely close to my face is beeping, and I wake up. At some point last night, somewhere in the midst of my insomniac wanderings, I must have headed back upstairs to the bedroom and fallen asleep in the bed, because that's where I am. The blanket fell on the floor and the room is freezing. I forgot to close the window. I pull in my legs and wrap my arms around my knees. *If only I could just get out of waking up one morning.* There's another beep, and I lazily reach over for my phone on the nightstand. The screen shows two new text messages from my sister. The first is four words long: You're coming tonight, right? The second message is just as succinct, but the tone is different: 7PM sharp!

I force myself out of bed, pull on my bathrobe, and go downstairs. The same motions, bathrobe, and stairs as yesterday and the day before. The same motions, bathrobe, and stairs that await me tomorrow and the day after that. In the kitchen I put on the kettle and make tea, not that it matters whether I eat breakfast, but because that's what one does, that's the way a person behaves. Plus it gives me something to fill my time and thoughts with. Something different.

I sit down and blow on my tea. Between sips, I stare out the window, my gaze roaming across the little landscaped yard between the houses. A few birds are chirping in a bush. In the kitchen of the place across from mine stands a man wearing a suit and tying his tie. At the table in front of him sits a woman with honey-colored hair, drinking something from a cup. The sun hasn't made it over the rooftops yet. A garbage truck chugs down the street. People hurry along the sidewalk. They're on their way somewhere. Their steps have direction and purpose.

I turn my attention to the room I find myself in, and behold its drab, bare appearance: the missing bits of wallpaper, the worn handles on the cupboard doors. The furnishings consist of a table and two simple chairs. Yet another day of empty motions and artificial respiration awaits within these four walls; yet another day of silence and solitude. My sister is my only remaining link to the outside world. This is what it's come to. This is what I've allowed it to come to. *You're coming tonight, right?* I get up from the table and dump out the rest of my tea in the sink. *I don't know,* I think. *I really don't know.*

2

My sister squats in front of the oven and peers through the dirty glass.

"It's done," she decides, adjusting the pot holders before opening the door.

A pan of lasagna lands on the table in front of me, alongside a simple green salad and red boxed wine. It's the same thing she's served the last several Fridays. She seems to like lasagna. Or maybe she's decided that I do? My sister holds up the box of wine and fills my glass first and then her own. After that she sits across from me and offers me the serving utensils.

"Go for it," she says.

Soon two steaming helpings sit on the plates in front of us. My sister has a healthy appetite. She says something about the weather, about how waiting for things to warm up in the spring is the worst. After having tried to start a discussion about some new TV show I've never heard of, she asks how I like my new place. I answer that I'm sure it will be fine but that I haven't really settled in yet.

My words sound stiff and fake. I feel that strangeness again, just like a few hours earlier when I stood in the front hall, just inside the door. I was dressed and ready to go out when this feeling of unreality came over me. *This won't do. I'm not up to this.* I realized that I was going to have to call and cancel, that I couldn't go to my sister's for our now-traditional Friday-night dinner. *Sit there eating and chatting, pretending as if everything is as it should be. No, not again. Never again.* And yet, in the end, here I am.

"Yes, yes," my sister says. "It's not like you owe it to me to be happy there just because."

The woman I'm subletting the place from is one of my sister's many friends. She's traveling around the world right now. That's the kind of thing my sister's friends do. They fly places and grab life by the horns. My sister and her husband used to travel, too—sometimes on their own and sometimes with other couples—but it's been a long time since they've done that.

"I mean, we're only talking about a few months," my sister says, and I realize that she's still talking about the town house, about my existence.

She rotates her wineglass in her hand, eyeing me thoughtfully. She had previously offered to let me live here, with her and her husband, and now I have the sense that she's about to repeat the invitation.

"I'll figure it out," I say in answer to a question that wasn't really asked.

Out of the corner of my eye, I think I catch my sister eyeing my plate and the food sitting there more or less untouched. I dutifully stuff a bite of lasagna into my mouth and wash it down with wine, not tasting it. Then I ask my sister a question about her job and listen as best I can while she answers. Things go better when we focus on her instead of me.

I empty my glass and my sister refills it. The alcohol does its part, dulling the sharp edges, dimming and covering. I feel almost real.

"How about you?" my sister asks after a while.

"What about me?"

"Have you started to give any thought to the future?"

I look down at my plate again, poking at the lettuce leaves. The future? The future is already behind me. That's what I think, even if I know better than to say it out loud. I make do with a simple shrug, but my sister doesn't relent. How's the writing going? Have I started anything new? I moisten my lips and tell it like it is.

My sister leans toward me.

"You need to get back to writing," she says firmly. "Work is the best medicine."

I stiffen. "Work is the best medicine" is Mama's old mantra. The words she smilingly used to counter all our efforts to make her rest, to not overdo it. The words she constantly repeated, right up until the pain made it impossible for her to speak, let alone sit up in bed and read or write.

My sister says the words so neutrally, as if they don't have any deeper significance to her. There's nothing in her voice to suggest that she remembers. Maybe she doesn't. By the time Mama got sick, she'd already been living away from home for a long time. She lived abroad for so long and rarely came home to visit until the final stage.

I fill my chest with air and hold it in. Only when my chest feels tight and my ribs ache, only when I no longer have any choice, do I exhale again.

"Just so you know, I am actually working pretty much all the time."

That's true. I accept as much work as I can as a publisher's reader and translator.

"It's great that you're busy, but you're an author, Elena. Authors write, right? They don't just dink around with other people's texts."

My glass is empty, again. I stare at the box of wine.

"I don't have anything to write about."

My sister pours me yet more wine and then gets up to fetch some ketchup from the fridge.

"What's that thing your publisher always says, that writing advice . . . dig your own grave, or something?"

A strange sound, which could have been a laugh, hacks its way from between my lips. My sister raises her eyebrows, and once again I look away. I suppose I'm getting a bit tipsy.

"Dig where you are," I correct her quietly.

"Right, that's the one," my sister says, picking up her fork and knife again. "Whatever. Anyway, I know you've mentioned the saying several times. So are you working on old manuscripts or what?"

I nod slowly. For the majority of my life, I've been a spectator, a person who observes rather than participates. This has benefited my writing. My texts have been based on events and developments I've either witnessed or heard tell of. The characters in my four books have all been based on people I've known, although that hasn't been evident to those involved. All an author needs to do is sprinkle in a few smoke screens— maybe change the character's age or profession—to keep people from recognizing themselves and realizing that the book is about them. I've written about friends and coworkers, about people I've known intimately but also about those I know only by sight. I've written about my mother and father, even my sister. I don't think she's aware of it.

"Do you remember," she says, breaking into a smile, "how I used to read your manuscripts before you sent them off? Especially in the beginning before you were published, but after that, too. At least for your first two books. You said I had really shrewd observations, and that I helped you bring out the best in the text."

Even though I had just set down my glass, I pick it up again. The wine runs down my throat, full-bodied and harsh.

"I'd love to do that again," my sister continues. "Read what you're writing, I mean."

I tell her there's a little ketchup on her chin, and as she dabs it with her napkin I say, "Like I said, there's nothing to read."

"But what about that advice? 'Dig where you are.' If that worked before, you could just follow it again, right?"

I lean back in my chair.

"Why is it so important to you?"

"Because I think you need something to really commit yourself to, something to focus on fully and completely while you go through . . . what you're going through."

We look at each other. Finally my sister throws up her hands and mumbles, "OK, OK." Then something else seems to occur to her. She passes the ketchup bottle to me and asks if I won't take a few more bites. Apparently I've barely touched my food.

I explain that I'm not hungry and push the plate away.

"Where's Walter tonight?" I ask, shifting the conversation away from me.

"Bowling, I think."

Up until now, I've taken it for granted that my sister and her husband have a good relationship. It has just seemed that way. Suddenly I don't feel so sure anymore. A married couple that spends every Friday night apart . . . isn't that a little odd? And then there's that business about the trips. Why have they stopped traveling together on weekends and vacations?

I study my sister more closely. Is there something she's not telling me? Maybe their relationship isn't that good after all.

"How's he doing? Have you guys—"

I'm interrupted by noise from the apartment upstairs—high-pitched voices and a series of howls followed by a thud.

"They just moved in," my sister says, flashing that wry smile that is so typically her. "Three children, all under the age of seven."

She rolls her eyes, and I pretend to follow her gaze, but I sneak a peek at her face, the arch of her forehead, the lines of her lips. The likeness is striking. I wonder if my sister is aware of it, if she sees whose features she's inherited when she looks in the mirror—and, if she does, what she thinks about it. If we had a different relationship, I could ask her, but now things are the way they are.

We hear another thud from the apartment above, this time fol-lowed by children's laughter and an adult's quiet voice. We can't make out the words, but it's obvious that the speaker is a warm, loving parent. I pull the back of my hand across my eyes. When I look up again, my sister has crumpled her napkin into a ball. She squeezes it in her hand and studies it intently.

"You know," she says, "it is possible to live a happy life without children."

Once again a sense of unreality sweeps in. Everything comes back to me, and at the same time I feel unmoored. My sister says something else—something about Walter and her and how they definitely chose this themselves, *but still*. She understands that it must be heartbreaking, *but still*.

"What I meant . . . and I'm sorry if I'm overstepping here, but are you really going to leave him for something like that? I mean, you love each other."

She puts her napkin on her plate with what's left of her food and looks me in the eye. Then she reaches across the table and rests her warm, slightly damp palm on the dry back of my hand. I stare at her fingers covering mine and think that even they remind me of Mama's. The lump in my throat grows, and I can't get a word out.

Finally my sister pulls her hand back, and she gets up to clear the dishes.

While she starts loading the dishwasher, I close my eyes and feel the world capsizing. *What am I doing here? Why did I even come?*

Soon the table is clear except for my empty wineglass. My sister closes the dishwasher.

"There's ice cream for dessert," she tells me.

As if in slow motion, I get to my feet, reach for my glass, and walk over to the sink. It takes every ounce of effort I have to keep from dropping the glass on the floor. Nausea shoots through my body, rolling over me in waves. Once I set my glass down, I turn to my sister.

"I think I'm going to call a cab," I say. "After all, tomorrow's another day."

3

The trip from my sister's apartment downtown to "my" place in the suburbs takes forty minutes by bus and less than half that by taxi. Cab rides are not a defensible expense based on my current financial situation, but I can't be bothered to care, not tonight.

I glance at the cabbie's dark curly hair and then look out the window and watch in silence as the city's lights flicker past.

I had blamed my early departure on exhaustion and nausea, told her I might be coming down with something. My sister didn't believe that at all. I could tell from her face, but she didn't say anything. We hugged before I left.

"See you next Friday," I mumbled into her hair before I hurried out to the waiting cab. "It'll be my turn to do dinner then."

The cab comes to a stop at a traffic light. The red light on my face changes to yellow and then green before we drive on.

It is possible to live a happy life without children. Are you really going to leave him for something like that?

There's so much my sister doesn't understand. To start with, she's never wanted to have children. But it's more than that between us, so much more than that. I remember our shared childhood, how it felt like the boundaries between us were fluid, as if my sister's essence were a part of me and vice versa. I remember a time when life was easy, when we were innocent, hopeful, the way children are. Then we grew up. My sister moved away from home, and everything changed.

If I had stayed and opened up to her tonight, if I'd told her about the insomnia and the emptiness and the confusion that is my existence without Peter, post-Peter.

But my sister and I don't go in for that kind of thing. We leave the piles of stones unturned. We leave unspoken words alone. Maybe she has her own reasons to maintain the distance between us, her own demons she's wrestling with. Or maybe it's all due to me, the twisted sister, the distorted mirror image.

The leather upholstery in the cab's backseat squeaks when I shift around, and the sour taste of wine rises in my throat. The cabbie signals and turns onto my block. The streetlights are broken here, and the lampposts stand like drooping, drowsy giants in the shadows along the side of the road. I stare into the night, feeling the darkness outside boring its way into me.

I take off my shoes and slip inside without turning on any lights. This is my home now and I'm entitled to be here, but I still feel like I'm trespassing. On a rational level, I'm aware of how lucky I am. This is a good house in a good neighborhood, and the terms of my sublet are almost painfully favorable. But as I move toward the kitchen, I feel like disapproving eyes stare at me from every direction, following me through the darkness.

The house doesn't want me here. Neither of us feels comfortable with the other, but you can't explain that kind of thing to your sister. She would blink uncomprehendingly at me, maybe shake her head and mutter something about nonsense. She would probably think I was being unappreciative, and if so, for good reason. My sister was the only one who knew of a place I could sublet on such short notice. Indeed, she was the only one I could even ask. I don't have any close friends left, and it's been several months since I've been in touch with any of the other freelancers I used to hang out with.

I stop in the kitchen doorway and peer into the room, which is also shrouded in darkness. The tabletop is empty apart from my computer. No one has made tea and put a cozy over the teapot to keep it warm until I came home. No one has made a couple of sandwiches or covered a slice of freshly baked pound cake with plastic wrap and set it on a plate in the fridge. And no one has left a note intended for me to read when I come home late from a trip to the library or maybe to hear an author read at some bookstore, a note with a loving greeting, words testifying to how much I mean to him.

I could boil a little water and make tea for myself. I could make some sandwiches or bake something, but it's not the same. And no matter what else I do to fool myself, it doesn't change the fact that no one leaves little notes for me, here, there, and everywhere—on the kitchen table, inside the bathroom cabinet, under the pillow. *A puzzle with only two pieces.*

I sit down on one of the two chairs, stare out the window, and try to keep my thoughts under control, try to prevent them from racing back in time. But looking forward isn't an option, either. The paths that used to be possible are all closed. The world has shrunk. Existence consists only of what I see around myself. What I should do is stand up and head for the bedroom. I should at least attempt to sleep. If I don't get up now, I may never do it. I may end up sitting here forever, a standing stone in the gloom. Perhaps I'll eventually crumble to pieces and disintegrate. Or else I'll be doomed to sit here staring out the kitchen window until one eternity ends and the next begins.

I become self-absorbed. The clock on the wall ticks, and the darkness deepens outside the window. It's as if I fade into a trance and it lasts right up until a movement out in the yard catches my eye. There's someone out there, a shadow figure at the fringes of the light cast by an old-fashioned streetlamp. An instant later, the light falls on a man on his way toward the house across the street. It must be the same man I saw in the kitchen over there earlier, the one who looked so elegant. But tonight his dark hair is disheveled, and the back of his suit jacket is wrinkly. He does something with his hands, straightens his pants or his shirt, maybe. His steps are hesitant, his feet drag on the ground. Suddenly he trips and looks like he's going to fall, but then he regains his balance and takes the final steps up to the house.

A strip of light from the second-floor window illuminates the façade of the building across from me as he puts his key into the front door. A figure with long hair—a woman in a nightgown—pulls back a heavy curtain and peers down at him. It only lasts a second, then the curtain falls back into place. The man opens the door and disappears inside.

The window pane in front of me goes dark again. I can make out the outlines of my own form in it, the faint reflection of a woman at a table. There's something uncanny about the image. I shiver and lean forward to lower the blinds. This motion gets me going, and I finally make it to my feet.

Enough of this, I think. Without really understanding what I mean by that.

4

THE HUSBAND

It's Friday night and I come home late, at a time when my wife will no doubt be asleep. Even so, I get it into my head that she's sitting up, waiting in there, that she's standing behind a curtain watching me. Maybe that's why I don't raise my face to look up at our bedroom window. I can't handle having her look me in the eye just now.

I feel self-confident but tense, checking one more time that my shirt is properly tucked in. Just before I reach the door, I trip and almost fall, then I regain my balance but still don't look up.

In the front hall, I hang up my jacket and put my shoes where they go. I move as quietly as I can and don't turn on the hallway light. Sometimes I sneak into the bathroom and rinse off, but usually I shower before I come home, at her place. Yes, I'm sleeping with a woman who isn't my wife. It's not something I'm proud of, but there it is. One could say that there are many reasons for it, and one could say there is only one reason.

The bedroom door is almost completely shut. It's only very slightly ajar. I cautiously push it open and then stand in the doorway for a couple of seconds until my eyes can see through the room's shadows. The contours of a body in the bed, the blanket rising and falling in time to the faint sound of regular breathing. Exactly as though she's sleeping. Why does it even occur to me that she isn't? Why do I imagine she's pretending? I tiptoe over to the bed, lift up the blanket, and slip in under it. The mattress complains under my weight, making me think of the body that moaned and groaned beneath me earlier. The blood pumps faster through my member as I remember.

I'm not going to lie. The sex is amazing, it is. A new body, with new lines and a new scent, new skin beneath my palms. The attraction is heady and raw. And yet what's going on between us has astonishingly little to do with sex—that part, I could do without. I know that sounds strange, but it's true.

It's like this: When we shut the door behind us, it's like leaving the world for a while. She touches me, and everything else disappears. For a while, I can forget. That's the feeling I can't do without.

Sometimes I feel pathetic. I *am* pathetic, if not even worse. That day when we got married, we were so sure then, so convinced that what we had was unique, that we weren't like other people. We would never allow our love to be sullied, never betray each other the way men and women have done from time immemorial. We were different. Our love was of a different sort. That was before I found out my wife's secret, before I cheated on her with someone else.

Now we lie here in the dark, each on our side of the mattress, breathing in time through the lies.

I close my eyes and wait for sleep to arrive. I occasionally dream that I tell my wife the truth. Everything feels so realistic in those dreams, just as if it were really happening, as if I were there and saying those actual words, unburdening myself. But then, when the dream gets to my wife's reaction, everything is torn apart. Each time, the same thing happens.

I never get to see her face after the revelation, never know what effect my words have on her.

I wake up from those dreams in a cold sweat, my pulse running rampant. I stare into the darkness for a while, then turn toward my wife, who is sleeping up against me, and feel the lines of her body under the blanket. How would she react if I told her, in reality?

I don't even dare imagine.

5

The day she decided to kill her husband was a Friday.

If anyone ever had the notion to write her story, that was maybe the moment to begin with.

But her tale consisted mostly of what had happened long before and what happened afterward. It consisted of things she did to herself and things she did to other people, a tale of blood and chaos, but also of words and thoughts.

"I will always love you. I will never leave you."

Words you say, that's all.

"I will cleave unto you and only you until death do us part."

Words you say, that's all.

I could kill that asshole.

Thoughts a woman has, that's all.

Or?

She decided to kill her husband on a Friday, but it took a while before her decision could be carried out. And that's not actually what the story was about.

It was about all the other stuff.

6

ELENA

Days come and go, added together like pearls on a string. The shades vary, but the color is always gray. No sun, no green leaves. I step outside the door only when it's necessary—to throw away the trash, sometimes to buy bread and milk. Otherwise I observe the changes in the light from my spot at the kitchen table. That's where I sit and work, where I set up my computer and spread out my notes. There's an office next to the kitchen, but the woman who owns the house, my sister's friend, stores most of her stuff in there and keeps the door locked. It doesn't matter. My life hardly takes up any space. The kitchen table is fine for the work I do.

I freelance for a publisher's reading service, where aspiring authors send their work to have it read and evaluated. The quality varies. Some manuscripts are compelling and well written. Others are incoherent and trite. This time I've received one of each. In both cases, my job is to explain informatively and concretely what works and what doesn't work, to discuss and give examples. It's challenging work. It requires attention and time, and it forces me to focus on something other than myself. Even if my sister doesn't seem to think it's enough. *Authors write, right? They don't just dink around with other people's texts.*

Every once in a while, my mind drifts off and I catch myself resting my chin in my hand, gazing out the window. The yard is pleasant and inviting, little flagstone paths wind their way through various types of bushes, and there's a garden bench that's been painted blue. And yet I never see anyone out there. I hardly ever see any of the neighbors at all, apart from the family across from me, whose kitchen I have an essentially unimpeded view into and thus occasionally catch a glimpse of.

"Don't expect anyone to come knock on your door and welcome you," my sister told me when she helped me move in.

This is not a place for people trying to meet people, she explained. This is a neighborhood for people who keep to themselves and prefer that others do the same. I was waiting for her to add *You'll fit in perfectly here*, but she didn't.

Beyond checking in about Friday dinners, she likes to text me, wondering how I'm doing and if I'm feeling better. I respond briefly to her messages. One time I did write a longer message, but I quickly lost my train of thought and stared at the words before erasing the whole thing again. Every sentence I write to her bugs me. Once, ages ago, she was closer to me than anyone else. Now we don't know anything about each other.

At night I lie awake. When my sheets are so damp and wrinkled that I can't stand it anymore, I get up and go downstairs where I yet again repeat my restless wandering between rooms. I drink water in the kitchen, then stand in front of the mirror in the bathroom and stare at myself. Sooner or later, I wind up in the living room in front of the bookshelf. I sort and re-sort, go from alphabetical by title to alphabetical by author, from color-coordinated spines to grouped by genre. And then back again.

Stories. In one way or another, they've always been my safe spot, the hub around which my life rotates. When we were little, Mama used to read aloud to us every night. We curled up on either side of her and listened raptly. It was the high point of the day. I loved the stories about princes and princesses who in their different ways were forced to fight to vanquish evil. My sister was six years older. I remember when she stopped being interested and started to pull away.

"I mean, they're just fairy tales," she said.

Mama put her arm around me and winked conspiratorially.

"Fairy tales are no trifling matter."

The read-aloud sessions of childhood gradually ebbed, but I kept reading on my own. The stories weren't just about heroes and heroines anymore, but about extremely real, imperfect people. The battles they waged were just as much against inner demons as against external threats.

"Just like real life," Mama said, tucking a lock of hair behind my ear.

Mama. I'm never so close to her as when I stand at the bookshelf. Even so, she's more distant now than ever before.

When Friday comes, I eat dinner at my sister's place again. It's actually my turn to have her over, but when I mumble that I haven't really had a chance to get settled in yet, my sister quickly says we can just do it at her place.

"What about Walter?" I ask.

She says it's fine.

I wonder if that means he's going to be home this time, that maybe he'll join us, but then it turns out not to be the case. Evidently he's out bowling again.

On the whole, this dinner is a repeat of the previous one. My sister does her best to get me to eat more.

"It's important that you eat, Elena, especially now."

She talks about an interview she heard on the radio, some author who had overcome writer's block after several years. He had a number of clever thoughts and suggestions apparently. She'll send me the link to the interview so I can listen to it later. She doesn't mention Peter, though, and when the children in the apartment upstairs are at their loudest, she quietly bites her lip and avoids making eye contact with me. Still, I know she wonders, wonders what this separation will lead to and how things will turn out for me and Peter, whether we'll really go our separate ways.

Don't you think I'm wondering the same thing? I feel like yelling at her. *Don't you think I ask myself every second of every day what the fuck I'm doing? Don't you understand that every minute, every hour without him feels like a lifetime? That I would do anything to turn back time, to be in his arms again? But this isn't about what I want. This is about our reaching a point where there was no longer any choice.* I don't say any of this out loud, or very much of anything else, either.

On Saturday morning, I'm back at the kitchen table. There's a dull buzzing in the back of my head, a sound that doesn't go away but does at least recede when I begin working. I open the two documents for the reader's report and start summarizing my opinions about the characters and the language, the plot and the narrative technique. When that's done, I take great pains with my concluding recommendations for the authors. In one case, I suggest some publishers to send the text to. In the other I encourage further revisions before taking that step. I email the reports to the agency and attach my invoice. Then I close the computer, lean back in the chair, and look out the window. *And now? What do I do now?*

The sky is hidden behind ominous clouds. The unreality intensifies the buzzing in the back of my head. On Monday morning, right when they open, I'll call the agency and see if they have more work for me. My sister is right about one thing. I need something to concentrate on, something to dig into, until the pain subsides. *And what if it never subsides?* I close my eyes and then open them again just as the light in the kitchen across the yard turns on.

The woman with the honey-colored hair comes in, wearing a white blouse and high-waisted pants. Her hair is up in a tight ponytail and she looks pretty put together, the way she usually does. The only time I've seen her otherwise was that night when she peeked down at her husband through the gap in the upstairs curtains. She walks over to the kitchen table now, over to a bouquet of flowers. It's a large armful of roses. They look like the long-stemmed variety. They extend above and beyond the edges of the vase, and their dark crimson color stands out in sharp contrast to the table, the kitchen cabinets, and the lamp, which are all a severe white. The woman with the ponytail tenderly touches the flower petals, leans over to smell them, and then starts arranging the stems. Every now and then she takes a step back and inspects the arrangement, but she doesn't seem satisfied, because she keeps fiddling with the flowers, really taking her time.

Eventually something else captures her attention. She turns her face toward the kitchen doorway. A couple of seconds later, the Suit Man reveals himself at the edge of my field of vision. I call him that because I have yet to see him wear anything else. He doesn't walk over to his wife but remains standing in the doorway. It looks like they exchange a few words, maybe he does most of the talking. After a few minutes, she turns back to the flowers, but her hands remain motionless in the middle of the bouquet.

My gaze returns to Suit Man. He's still there, but there's something indecisive about his body language. Then he takes a few steps forward and quickly kisses his wife's cheek before leaving. The front door opens, and he emerges with a briefcase in one hand and a carry-on bag in the other. Only now do I notice the taxi waiting by the curb. Suit Man lets the cabbie deal with his bag and seats himself in the backseat with his briefcase. His wife stands at the kitchen window and watches him. Her face is like an open wound.

When the taxi pulls away, her expression changes and she turns her back to me. She seems to be looking for something over by the sink, and when she turns around again, she's holding a large pair of scissors. A second later she raises the scissors and aims a powerful chop at the roses. I stiffen. She does the same thing again, and yet again. She slices through more and more stems, and red petals rain down. The woman's face is blotchy and her motions furious. I'm transfixed, unable to move from this spot. All I can do is watch as she continues slaughtering the bouquet, alternating between the scissors and her own hands. She chops, cuts, and rips apart the flowers.

She doesn't stop until every flower is completely destroyed. Then she tosses aside the scissors and clutches her head in both hands, squeezes her eyes closed, and opens her mouth wide. The sound of her scream doesn't reach me, but I can clearly see her entire body vibrating. I wrap my hands around my upper arms and hug myself. My palms are ice-cold.

The scream appears to give way to crying as the woman slumps onto a chair, her face falling to the table and disappearing from my line of sight. I remain motionless for a few minutes, waiting for her next move, but all I can see is part of her high ponytail sticking up over the bottom edge of the window. Then it's suddenly as if the kitchen across from me recedes, as if I'm watching it from the other end of a tunnel. That strange sense—intense presence blended with strong oversensitivity—comes over me again. *Dig where you are.*

My eyes fall to the computer in front of me. My fingers move of their own accord, opening a new document, finding their way across the keyboard. Sentence is added to sentence. It's as foreign to me as it is straightforward. *Authors write, right?* And I'm writing, I really am now. For the first time in ages I'm writing something of my own, something new. This insight leaves me with an effervescent feeling.

When I look up, I can no longer see any ponytail. The woman appears to have left the room. Only the massacred roses remain. I feel a sense of urgency. I turn my attention back to the screen and read what I just wrote, then glance over at the kitchen across the yard and then back at what I'm writing again. What am I going to do with this? Where is this going? I stare at the blinking cursor. All I need to do is select all and hit delete. *Just do it now, forget it and move on.*

I raise my hand. My fingers hover in the air for a moment before they hit the keyboard. But they don't hit delete. They hit save.

7

How did it happen? It's impossible to say.

Suddenly she was just holding the scissors in her hand.

A moment later, the flowers had been abused and shredded and strewn across the floor.

Afterward, she had nothing other than disconnected memories of what had happened. She remembered the thorns that had torn up her skin, and the red streaks etched over the thin blue veins in her forearms. She remembered the uncontrolled roar that forced its way out of her throat.

A noise an animal might sooner make than a scream.

It hadn't contained any words, and yet she knew exactly what it meant.

"You bastard. You're next."

8

ELENA

No, there are no new jobs available at the moment. My contact at the agency sounds almost amused when I call at 8:01 on Monday morning to find out if they have any more manuscripts they need read.

"You just finished two manuscripts, Elena. I'm looking at your email now, and everything looks great. As usual."

He says that they went through a large batch of manuscripts on Friday and divvied them up to a handful of readers. But since I had two other open projects then, they chose to place them with other freelancers this time.

"You're one of our hardest-working readers, Elena. I'm sure you could use a break every now and then, right?"

I have to bite my lip to keep from screaming. *What I need is something to fill my time and occupy my mind, something to stave off the effects of idleness and passivity. I don't need to take time off. I need to keep the worried turbulence inside me in check.*

But of course the man at the agency knows none of this.

"Take a walk in the city," he advises me. "Go meet a friend for coffee. You can do that kind of thing when you work freelance. Call back next Monday, and we'll see what's come in by then."

I ask him to keep me in mind if anything should happen to pop up in the meantime. I force myself to sound calm, but when I hang up, I'm cringing. *Next Monday?* There's a vast ocean of time between now and then. What am I going to do with myself until then?

I take a bite of my sandwich and look out the window just as the woman with the ponytail walks out her front door and across the yard. She is wearing an elegant coat and a pair of dark sunglasses that cover half her face. She looks like an old-fashioned movie star, cool and collected. *But I saw you,* flashes through my head, *I saw you go berserk on those flowers.* I watch until she disappears around the corner. At some point during the day yesterday, Suit Man must have returned from his trip, because he also left the house a little while ago, around the time when I walked into the kitchen. His back straight and his shoes highly polished, he hurried out to the street, holding tight to his briefcase. He looked stressed out, like an important man on his way to deal with important matters. The complete antithesis of me.

My sandwich tastes like nothing, and I toss the rest in the trash and get up from the table. What was it the man at the agency recommended— going for a walk?

I pull on a pair of worn pants, a soft long-sleeved top, and a down vest. Then I'm suddenly standing outside the house for the first time in several days, and I'm looking around. There's not a person in sight. The shared green space is empty, the town houses curve around its periphery like one long contiguous body composed of huddled, slumbering house creatures. I slowly make my way along the path that cuts across the grass. I should head left toward the street. There's no reason to keep going straight, past the bushes and trash cans. And yet, that's what I do.

Before I know it, I'm standing in front of the house across from mine. There's a black sign attached at eye level right beside the front door: **THE STORMS.**

I can't explain what happens next, only know that suddenly I've opened a search page on my phone and entered the address. It only takes a second for the results to appear. There are three people listed at this address, Philip, Veronica, and Leo Storm. In other words, there's a child in the household, a son. I nod to myself, recalling that I've seen a boy walking toward the house a few times. I'd guess him to be about twelve years old. I noticed him because the backpack he wore over his narrow shoulders looked so heavy and unwieldy.

I do a new search for Philip Storm. At the top of the search results, there's a link to a corporate law firm's sober-looking home page. I click on "Meet Our Team," and a photo of the man in the house across from me pops up. Under his picture, it says "Attorney" and "Partner." I'm about to do yet another search, this time for Veronica Storm, when I hear a scraping sound somewhere very nearby. I stiffen and realize that I'm no longer alone. Someone is standing behind me.

I turn around and am looking into the eyes of an elderly woman with a hunched back. I can't recall having seen her before, but she's wearing what looks like a bathrobe, so I assume she's actually one of my neighbors. I attempt a smile, which she does not return. Instead she studies me with suspicion and I quickly realize how close I am to the Storm family's house and how strange it must look that I'm just standing here staring.

I open my mouth and hear myself going on and on, saying that I've just moved in and that I feel like there's something familiar about the family in the house across from mine. Each word sounds more forced than the last, and before I've gone as far as introducing myself and shaking hands, the old woman simply turns her back to me and shuffles away to one of the houses farther down. I'm left standing there with a sense of having been caught red-handed doing something scandalous.

I glance toward my own kitchen window. I'm tempted to hurry back home, but then I remind myself what awaits me: absolutely nothing. Somehow I have to make it through the days until I get more work. I need to distract my mind and tire out my body.

I pull up the zipper on my vest and start walking.

An hour and a half later, I'm downtown. My legs are numb, and there's a blister developing on my heel. I'm hungry, and even thirstier. There's a bakery where I sometimes go to write. It's cozy but a little out of the way, which means walking for another ten or fifteen minutes. I'm not sure I'm up to that. I slow my pace and stop in front of a high-rise. Still trying to make up my mind, I lift my face to take in the façade in front of me. That's when I see it—the sign bearing the name of a familiar company, the name of a law firm: Philip Storm's office.

9

Incredulously I stare at the sign bearing the company name. Of all the intersections in the city, how did I end up at this one? Had I remembered the address? Did I somehow subconsciously navigate my way here? And if so, why?

I look around, spot a café across the street, and realize once again how thirsty I am. Plus my legs could really use a rest. Now that I'm here, there's not really much point in dwelling on why I came this way. I cross the street and enter the café, order chicken salad and mineral water, and sit down at one of the tables closest to the window. *I should probably have settled for tap water,* I think as the bubbly liquid pours out of the bottle and into the glass. I'm still living on the money from my last book, the only one of the four books I've written to date that became a commercial success, but my royalties will be drying up soon. And the editorial gigs don't pay all that much. Especially when I don't even have any to work on. I poke at the pieces of chicken and romaine with my fork, and despite having been so hungry just a minute ago, I quickly lose my appetite.

I put down my silverware, push the plate away, and lean back. This motion causes one of my chair legs to scrape loudly against the floor. A man at a table across the room looks up from his computer, and from the corner a few teenage girls giggle loudly. My cheeks flush, and suddenly I feel like everyone is staring at me. I feel transparent, as if every thought and every emotion inside me is visible.

Out of the corner of my eye, I see the man turn his attention back to his computer, and I regret not having brought my own computer. That's what normal people do. They keep themselves busy, look like they're doing something. Feeling unsettled, I drink the last of my mineral water and wonder if I would do better to walk back home or if I should maybe take the bus. But then my sister calls. She's at work, between meetings, and is calling to talk about what we're going to do for Papa's birthday, which is this week already. Should we send a card or not? *Papa*. The muscles in my face stiffen.

Mama's coffin was hardly in the ground before Papa met a new woman and moved north with her. In the years since then, he hasn't shown much interest in getting together with my sister or me. When he does occasionally get in touch, it's with a postcard depicting an active, outdoorsy life. The kind of life he'd probably always dreamed of but didn't really have a chance to pursue with Mama. While she enjoyed her quiet life surrounded by her books, he was an active person who became restless when he had to sit for long periods.

One of his favorite sports was skiing, and I remember when I turned five or six how he taught me downhill skiing on the little neighborhood sledding hill. He set up a long line of ski poles down the side of the hill, then pulled me up to the top and let me ski down the slope over and over again. A few of the other fathers teased him, laughing at how he schlepped me up the hill again and again, but he didn't care about that. He was tireless in his efforts.

On the phone, my sister vacillates. I listen to the various arguments for and against getting a card as my gaze drifts out the window to the intersection. I haven't been skiing in years. I'll probably never want to do anything that reminds me of Papa again, just as he seems content not to have been reminded of my existence any more than necessary.

I'm about to tell my sister that, as far as I'm concerned, we can skip the birthday card, when I spot a familiar face. Philip Storm steps out of his building and strides quickly down the sidewalk. My back straightens, as if on its own.

"Hey, can we talk about this later?" I say, standing up. "I'm kind of in a hurry."

My vest is hanging over the back of my chair. I grab it and hurry out the door. My sister can't conceal her surprise.

"In a hurry? For what?"

That's a question I don't care to try to answer, so I just hang up.

I cross the street and hurry after Philip Storm. Despite my stiff joints and sore muscles, I soon catch up to him. His phone is pressed to his ear as he obviously talks to someone. When he turns a corner and crosses yet another street, I do the same.

Am I following him? Is that what I'm doing? If I am, I convince myself, it's inadvertent. He'll soon reach the restaurant he's surely heading to for lunch, meet up with whomever he's meeting—probably a bunch of people in suits—and vanish into a murmur of voices and the smell of fried food. Then I'll continue down the sidewalk, passing by without slowing or even turning my head. I'll walk until I reach a stop for the right bus, wait for the next one, ride it home, and shut myself in and not go out again for a very long time. Not until it's necessary.

But no. We pass several different restaurants, and Philip Storm doesn't stop at any of them. He's removed his hand from his ear and put his phone in his pocket. Has he sped up as well? There's eagerness and tension to his steps. Finally he turns onto a small cross street with neither car traffic nor restaurants. A red-haired woman in a tight knit dress is standing outside a door on the right side, smoking. She isn't wearing a coat and obviously works or lives on the block. When she sees Philip, she straightens up and puts out her cigarette. I linger at the corner, pretending to study an ad posted in the window of a real estate agency, as I observe them from a distance.

Philip Storm stops in front of the red-haired woman. The distance between their bodies can't be more than a couple of yards. They're close enough that I can hear that he sounds cheerful, and she laughs quietly in response. She puts a hand on his arm, and it looks like he's about to hug her, but then he stops. He hastily looks around instead, as if he's afraid someone will see them together. A second later, they're gone, in through a doorway. I turn around and stare at the door, which is just closing behind them. *What if I hurried over there and managed to grab it before it closed all the way? What if I surprised the two of them in there when they thought they were finally alone, shielded from the world's prying eyes? What would I see?*

The bus ride home is bumpy. My stomach lurches. Something comes loose and bubbles up into my chest. The bus driver brakes again abruptly. I don't feel well. Maybe it's motion sickness, maybe something else entirely.

10

All these phone calls. The ones that took place before she knew.

He called to say that he needed to finish something at work and would be home late. Or to share the details of yet another business trip that he needed to go on.

But most of all, of course, she was the one who called. She called to find out how his day was going, to ask if he wanted to meet spontaneously for lunch or quite simply to get his opinion on some practical question.

All the times he didn't have time to talk, was in a bind, when it wasn't a good time. All the times he didn't pick up at all.

Sometimes she caught him on his way somewhere. She could make out the sounds of traffic and city life in the background and imagined him having just left his office. She could picture him walking down the sidewalk, his phone pressed to his ear. "Where are you going?" she usually asked. Did he ever answer that?

All the phone calls in the years they'd been married: "See you later. Don't forget to buy milk. Bye, love ya." One of those conversations became the last.

The last call before everything fell apart.

The last call before the beast within her awoke.

11

THE HUSBAND

I've never been good at being alone, have always been too fond of having someone by my side. The single life never appealed to me. I've been in one relationship or another, with very few breaks in between, ever since I lost my virginity at the age of seventeen. Different women, but only one at a time—until now, that is. There are two women in my life now: my wife and Anna.

We've started meeting more frequently, less and less often at a hotel and more often at her place. We still fall into bed as soon as we close the door behind us. But afterward, we talk more, and for longer. We often laugh, and she cried once. Each time it feels a little weirder to get dressed and return to reality, where we mean nothing at all to each other. It's like living in parallel universes.

Today, as I was heading to our date, my wife called. She asked where I was and when I would be home. I hate lying, hate going behind people's backs. I feel an urgent need to tell her what's going on. But what actually *is* going on between Anna and me? My head is throbbing. All I know is that it can't continue like this.

I think back to a TV series we used to watch when we were still happy newlyweds. It feels like ages ago, but there's still one line that is indelibly etched in my memory . . . "Hell hath no fury like a woman scorned." Apparently it's a literary quote, but I'd never heard it, and I remember that I laughed, and thought it was quite ingenious. But no matter how I try, I can't remember my wife's reaction. It was before she told me the terrible news. Otherwise I'd remember, I'm sure of it.

In hindsight, it's impossible to ignore the fact that she didn't tell me until after we were already married. I can't help but wonder why, can't help but wonder whether she consciously wanted to wait until we were legally bound together before she released her secret from the darkness. For all the days and nights before then, she'd been keeping something like that inside herself, concealed from me, the person she said she loved most. I still have a hard time fathoming it, making it fit with the image I have, or had, of our relationship. I thought we could talk about everything.

Sometimes, especially in the beginning, we would end up discussing our previous relationships and what had gone wrong in them. She mentioned her first love—of course she did, said that she was both disappointed and heartbroken. I remember interpreting it as a touching, although very classic, story of young heartache. There was no innuendo of anything else, not then. As I said, she waited until later to reveal the rest.

I pull my hands though Anna's hair, press her naked body tightly to my own . . . but something has happened. The protective filter between us and everything else is being chipped away. It's no longer so easy to forget the outside world. I am having more and more trouble not thinking about my wife when I'm with Anna. I'm haunted by my guilty conscience. Of course I feel guilty, but there's something else, too. It's related to the story my wife finally revealed—the story of what happened when she was younger, how she drove herself beyond all limits, went beyond everything that common sense dictates and everything that physical pain entails in order to seek revenge.

Hell hath no fury like a woman scorned.

I close my eyes and hold the woman in my arms even closer.

How will this turn out? How will this turn out for all of us?

12

ELENA

I'm writing. So far it's only fragments without any clear coherence or chronological order, but I'm writing. I start immediately after the bus ride home from downtown. It goes slowly at first. I'm far too self-aware, far too distanced. Then something happens. The text sucks me in, hits a nerve. My fingers move over the keyboard on their own, as if they can't work fast enough. I sit at the kitchen table with the blinds drawn but angled so the afternoon light can find its way in, and time slips away without my noticing it.

When the doorbell rings, I have no idea what I'm hearing. No one has used it before. I look up and see someone standing outside, only partially visible through the gaps between the blinds. It's not my sister. I get up and walk to the front door, checking my hair as I pass the mirror in the front hall. For once I'm properly dressed, thanks to my morning adventure. At least I pass some sort of threshold of common decency for when it's OK to open the door.

He is wearing a red hoodie and worn jeans, with a full backpack slung over one shoulder. At first he raises his hand to greet me, then changes his mind and holds it out to me. His palm is sweaty, but his grip is firm.

"Hi, I'm Leo. Leo Storm."

It's him, the son of the family who lives across from me. He's slim, if not downright skinny, and quite a bit shorter than I am. But he's older than twelve—that's clear now that I'm seeing him close up. There's something about the look in his eyes. Thirteen is a better guess, maybe even fourteen.

"I came home early. My mom's not home from work yet, and since I forgot my key, I was thinking maybe I should come introduce myself. You just moved in, right? I hope I'm not bothering you."

He turns around and points.

"I live in that house over there, across the yard."

I say my name, but my voice is hoarse from disuse and I have to clear my throat and try again. Leo nods.

"So you're an author, huh?"

Then he mentions the title of my latest book, the one that, after I released three books with unremarkable sales numbers, became an unexpected hit. Like my earlier works, my fourth thriller was a dark tale. The story revolved around a family that was falling apart, exploring what they were prepared to do to each other. The reviews used words like "unique" and "first class." I was invited to discuss the death of the nuclear family on TV, and the book raced up the bestseller list, appealing apparently to both suspense fans and readers of more traditional novels.

For a few months, people would recognize me in town, but that passed quickly, thank goodness. New books were always flooding the market, new authors sitting down on the morning-talk-show sofas and being featured in the books section of the paper. The spotlight went out, and I welcomed that, returning to my role as an observer, which is the role that makes me the most comfortable.

I'm not on social media, and my books are hardly targeted for teens. And yet this boy knows who I am. Apparently my confusion is evident.

"I hang out at the library a lot," Leo explains. "I'm, like, a major reader, so I keep track of stuff."

His bangs are long and hang down over his face. When he tosses his head, flinging his hair to the side, I get a glimpse of the skin on his forehead. It's covered with red and white zits.

"I hope it's OK that I came by. We don't usually knock on just anyone's door around here, and I don't want to bother you. It's just that I . . . well, I kind of . . ."

He pushes the long bangs off his forehead and then immediately lets them fall down again, using both his unconscious reaction to having his hair in his eyes and his conscious strategy of hiding his zits. An emotion I can't explain seizes hold of me.

"Don't worry," I say. "You're not bothering me."

"Are you sure?"

"I'm sure."

He looks down at his feet, at his carelessly tied, dirty white sneakers. Then he looks up again and meets my gaze from under his bangs.

"I want to be an author, too. When I grow up, I mean."

"Really? How exciting."

He tells me that he writes a fair amount on his computer at home, mostly short stories and shorter texts, everyday observations. And then, as he said, he reads a ton. He gestures toward his backpack and explains that it's not only full of schoolbooks but also a stack from the library.

"I have such a hard time choosing. I always check out too many."

"I was like that," I say. "Always starting a new book. Or five."

Leo laughs a little and asks what my parents thought about it. When I explain that my mother was the same way, that my interest came from her, he looks down again. His smile disappears.

"My dad thinks I ought to do more sports and read less. And the guys in my class, they don't understand why anyone would read anything if they didn't have to. They say I'm a fucking wuss who always—"

He stops midsentence, runs his hand under his bangs, and then straightens his backpack.

"Well, I guess I ought to . . ."

He speaks slowly, drawing out the words. I want to say something but don't know what, then the next moment, I've lost my chance. Leo is already on his way.

"I'll leave you alone now," he says. "See you."

"Good luck with the writing. And let me know if there's anything I can help you with."

His eyes widen.

"Really? That's awesome! Thanks."

We say goodbye. I shut my door and lean back against it. *Why did I have to throw out that last bit and give him room for hope?* I already know I won't live up to it. How can I help that boy when I'm only barely keeping it together myself?

Then it hits me. *Didn't he say he didn't have a key? And that neither of his parents was home yet? What does he think he's going to do—sit outside and wait for them?* The temperature drops rapidly this late in the afternoon, and I think his red hoodie doesn't look very warm.

I hesitate, and just as I reach to open the door again, my phone rings in the kitchen. I promise myself I'll check on him after I take the call, but I forget all about Leo Storm the second I see the caller ID: A name, just five letters, is all it takes to turn everything on its head. Because the caller is the love of my life, the man I haven't spoken to for five weeks and two days, and whom I've missed every second since then: *Peter.*

I don't know how many rings it takes for me to get hold of myself— two, three, five? But just before my trembling index finger can press the button to answer, the phone goes silent. Its screen goes black, and the phone is cold and lifeless in my hand. I slump down onto one of the kitchen chairs, stretch out my arms in front of me, and press my palms against the tabletop, realizing that otherwise I might collapse right out of the chair, collapse through the floor, down into empty nothingness.

13

Philip Storm steps out of the pale morning fog and lingers for a few seconds outside his front door. He stuffs something into his briefcase before he hurries off across the green space. The same shiny shoes as usual, the same self-confident bearing. His wife is still sitting at the kitchen table inside. Her face is turned toward the window, and she follows Philip's back with her eyes. The expression on her face is anything but loving, though. There's something about her expression, how she's staring at her husband . . . I chew a fingernail, trying to put my finger on what emotion she's radiating, but I don't succeed. My mind is far too foggy after yet another night of sleepless hours. I spent them wandering around and sorting books, my thoughts racing like wild animals within me.

We wouldn't contact each other at all, that was the agreement Peter and I had made: three months' trial separation, and only in exceptional cases would we get in touch if anything out of the ordinary happened—or if one of us reached a decision on how we wanted to proceed. Alone or together, divorce or reunite. Just over a month had passed, and neither of us had gotten in touch until yesterday.

The questions tore at me as I moved around in the night's shadows, feeling alternately cold and hot. Ultimately I decided it must have been a mistake and that Peter's name in my call log was nothing to worry about, nothing I could allow myself to feel hopeful about. Then I fell into some form of spasmodic, dreamless sleep before waking up again only a few hours later, and now I'm sitting here, in my bathrobe with my tangled hair, unable to even fix myself breakfast.

The next time the door across the way opens, it's the wife's turn to come out. Veronica. She turns around to lock her door, but I can still picture her face the way it looked an hour ago. I blink and enlarge the mental picture for myself. Its focus improves. I zoom in on every little muscle, every feature, and finally the picture is as clear as if she were standing beside me. A black fire burns in her eyes as they follow Philip across the yard. Is it rage? Or hatred? I open my eyes just as the bottom of her coat flaps and disappears around the corner. She's gone, but that nagging sensation inside me is still there.

I stand up and stretch, then walk over to the fridge but change my mind and return to the kitchen table. I sit down again and drum my fingers on the tabletop. I need something to do, but I won't see any new reading or editing gigs until Monday. There's also obviously a lull in the translation industry, too. I take out my computer and open the document with the text I started, but the letters swim before my eyes and there's a lump in my stomach.

I take out my phone and weigh it in my hand. *What if I sent Peter a text? What if I just laid it out and said exactly what I'm feeling?*

Without you I'm just a shell, an empty husk.

No! I toss my phone aside with so much force that it slips over the edge of the table and lands on the floor. The glass cracks, but the phone still works—unlike me. The crack through me runs much deeper, eating its way far below the surface.

I get up again and go out into the living room to sort the books on the shelf, even though it's the middle of the day. Then I'm so exhausted that I fall asleep and don't wake up again until many hours later, when my sister calls. It's obvious that I was asleep and that she woke me up, but I still claim otherwise. I say I've been up for ages, that I'm a little hoarse and maybe I'm coming down with a cold.

My sister is quiet for a second. It's as if she's gathering her strength to say something important, and I get it into my head that she's planning to give me some sort of warning or maybe reveal some secret. Like what's actually up with Walter and his bowling? But then I hear the sound of other people approaching. My sister works in one of those open-plan offices. She clears her throat. In a neutral tone, she says that she bought Papa a birthday card, wrote a greeting, and signed both our names. The card is nothing special, no balloons or hearts or anything like that. If that's OK with me, then she'll send it on her way home from work. I say that's fine.

Once again she speaks hesitantly, lowering her voice.

"Elena, have you eaten anything today?"

Before I have a chance to answer, someone in the background yells to my sister.

"OK, I have a meeting now," she says quickly. "We'll talk later."

I roll onto my side and feel my pulse speed up. She's coming here on Friday. I invited her. I have three days. My thoughts chase me out of bed, drive me back down to the living room. I stand there in the doorway and look around at the piles of brown moving boxes. The only furniture aside from the bookshelf is a worn sofa. Otherwise the room is a gaping, empty wasteland.

I proceed into the kitchen and subject it to the same thorough scrutiny. Two simple chairs, a rickety table, and a clock. That's it. Otherwise the walls and windows in here are bare. Not a painting as far as the eye can see, no live plants. Even my sister will think this place looks frightful. I need to show her that I'm making progress, and I have to increase the lived-in look at least slightly before she comes over. A part of me can't comprehend that I'm thinking these thoughts, dwelling on such trivial, insignificant things. Another part reminds me that it's my only chance, my only path forward.

A few hours later, when I'm on my way home from the flower shop, my sister calls again. I'd popped into the convenience store, too, only to realize that if I'm going to pull off a proper Friday dinner, I was going to need to do my shopping at a bigger grocery store. But that'll have to wait for another day. I fumble with the bags and bring my phone to my ear.

"Hello?"

"There's one other thing, too. One thing I need to . . ."

She was somewhere quiet now. Maybe she went into a conference room and closed the door so she could make the call in peace this time.

"Although I don't really know how to . . . or if this is the best way to . . ."

I was right. She does want to tell me something, and judging from the tension in her voice, it's a sensitive subject.

"I'm listening," I say.

At that moment I think, *Here it comes: Walter.*

But when my sister starts talking again, she's not talking about her husband. She's not even talking about herself. It's me. She says she's been thinking and that she feels like she was too hard on me last Friday with all that talk about how I had to get back to writing and how you can live a happy life without kids. Given that I hadn't asked what she thought, much less for her advice.

"Don't worry," I say when she stops. "I know you mean well."

"But that's exactly what I do—worry, I mean."

I clutch the paper bag more tightly, the one containing what the florist assured me were "easy-to-care-for plants."

"What do you mean?"

I'm almost home now, and the shared yard opens up before me. Leo is sitting outside his house with his head down, reading a book he holds in his lap. He sees me and waves. I wave back as my sister sighs on the other end of the line.

"Like food for example. You're an adult, Elena, and I have no right to . . . But you have to understand that I worry that it will happen again."

There is a faint whistling in my ears.

"That what will happen again?"

Leo has gathered up his things and is walking toward me now.

"Don't be mad now, but I know," my sister says.

I force myself to focus on my breathing, force myself to breathe as slowly as I can, in and out, in and out.

"Know what? What are you talking about?"

"I'm talking about the anorexia you had as a teenager." She stops for a second and then adds, "Mama told me."

The whistling in my ears increases in strength, and the last of the strength runs out of my arms. I have to set my bags on the ground. Leo, who has reached me now, points and gestures silently, asking if I want help carrying them. I shake my head, then exert intense effort to find my voice.

"I have to go now," I tell my sister. "Talk to you later."

"No, please," my sister wails, "don't do that. I didn't mean to just blurt it out like that, but I'm not very good at . . . I mean we don't usually . . . If you want, I can come over after work. Then we can sit down and talk, just you and me."

Leo shows that he understands I'm busy and that he's going to go back over to his place.

"No, wait!" I say.

Leo stops and gives me a questioning look.

"Are you talking to me?" my sister asks.

"Look," I say. "I'm busy. One of the neighbors just stopped by."

Then I hang up and put away my phone. I let a second or two go by before I raise my eyes to Leo. He's not wearing a jacket.

"Don't you get cold sitting out here wearing just that?"

He shrugs.

"You didn't forget your key again, did you?"

"I'm the world's biggest airhead, I know."

I look down into my bags, at the plants and the pots that are visible, and then I look at Leo's hands. His fingers are pale, almost blueish. He's obviously cold. I may have several options right now, but only one of them is the right thing to do.

I look up, and my eyes meet Leo's.

"Do you want to come in for a bit?"

14

When we're in the front hall, Leo opens his backpack to stuff in the book he was reading, and a piece of paper falls on the floor. It must have been tucked into the pages of his book. Now it's lying on the floor between us. It's scrawled in all caps, and it's impossible for me not to see what it says:

"LEO STORM = TOO UGLY TO EXIST!"

Leo stiffens, then he quickly bends down, grabs the paper, crumples it up, and crams it into his pocket.

"What was that?"

"Nothing."

He straightens up but won't look me in the eye. We head into the kitchen, and I tell Leo to have a seat while I put away the food and deal with my newly purchased plants. Instead he offers to help me, and soon we're busy potting, watering, and arranging the plants along the windowsill. When Leo turns toward the window to set a fern on the sill and then leans over to adjust its fronds, I sneak a peek at him. I can't shake the thought of that slip of paper. Did he write that about himself? Or was that a note from someone else?

Leo turns around and catches me looking. I quickly ask if he's hungry. A few minutes later, we're sitting at the table with a plate of oat crackers between us. Leo inhales several of them but is careful to leave half of the crackers for me. I shake my head, push the plate toward him, and tell him the truth: "*I'm* not hungry."

My sister's words echo in my ears: *The anorexia you had as a teenager. Mama told me.* I push my fingers together and feel the distaste—which had been temporarily displaced by thoughts of Leo—stir again. Had that conversation really taken place? And if so, what exactly had my mother told my sister?

Leo breaks the last cracker in half and crunches away on one half while he looks around at the kitchen.

"Do you live here by yourself?"

That question is unexpected, and I don't have time to think it over. A nod would have been enough, a simple *yes*, and yet the words pour out of me on their own.

"My husband and I are separated."

"Are you going to get divorced?" Leo asks seriously.

"We're living apart to have time to think on our own, but we're still married."

He nods and chews the last piece of cracker in silence. Once he's done, he brushes some small crumbs off the table into the palm of his hand.

"About that . . ." He sucks on his lip and nods toward the front hall before adding, ". . . note."

I nod slowly, waiting.

Leo tosses the remaining crumbs into his mouth and takes his time swallowing them.

"If you happen to meet my mom or dad, maybe say hello and start chatting or . . . Anyway, if you do, you don't need to mention that to them, the note, I mean."

I get up to fetch two glasses of water. I set one in front of Leo and sit back down in the chair across from him.

"Maybe *you* should tell them."

He doesn't respond.

"If things aren't going well," I continue, "if someone's picking on you . . ."

Leo shakes his head vigorously.

"My dad is busy. He works all the time and doesn't have time for things like that."

Things like that? I drink my water.

"Your mom, then?"

"My mom?"

Leo once again shakes his head so his bangs whip across his face.

"She wouldn't believe me."

Those words hang between us. Something fills the room, a new and different energy.

I keep my voice as indifferent as possible, trying to hide my curiosity. "Why do you say that?"

He glances furtively at the glass I set in front of him.

"My mom is . . . She's kind of . . ."

And then, right then, it's just there, that same sinking feeling I've had so many times before in various contexts and with widely differing people: *There's a story here.*

"What? She's what?"

Leo slowly raises his face. A look flits through his eyes, but it happens so quickly I don't have a chance to determine what it means.

"It's hard to explain," he mumbles, turning away again. "She's unique."

"How so? Can you give an example?"

That's going too far. I realize that as soon as I've asked the question, and I open my mouth to smooth it over, take it back. But Leo beats me to it.

"I remember," he mumbles, "this one time when I was little, maybe five or six. My mom and I were walking over a bridge, and suddenly she threw her purse over the side, just like that. I don't know where we'd been or where we were going, but I remember thinking it was weird that she was walking so close to the edge. We were holding hands, and I said something, but she didn't look at me, just kept staring at the water below. Then she raised her arm and threw her purse with her wallet, keys, phone, and everything in it. A man came and tried to help. He stuck a long branch down and tried to fish out the purse, but it didn't work. In the end, it sank. Later, when my mother went to explain what had happened to my father, I heard her use the word 'dropped,' and I remember how astonished I was. I mean, I knew she'd thrown that purse on purpose. I couldn't understand why she wouldn't just tell the truth, not even to Dad."

The kitchen clock ticks in the background, and Leo cracks his knuckles. I sit there dumbfounded. I don't know exactly what I was expecting, but hardly that he would tell me, someone he had only just met, something so private.

"You know, sometimes grown-ups do things that seem strange. That doesn't necessarily mean that . . ."

Leo looks up.

"That's just one story. I have more. There are worse things I could tell you—much worse."

"About your mother?"

"Yes, about my mother."

My thoughts go back to witnessing Veronica brandishing those scissors, the uncontrolled craziness of her motions. *More stories like that, and worse?* Then I stop and glance at him. *Doesn't it feel a little . . . well, a little desperate for a boy his age to open up like this to a stranger?* I shake my head, shaking away my questions about why he's doing it. The reason doesn't matter. Leo is young and maybe a little indiscreet. It's my responsibility to not exploit that.

I change the subject. And not long after that, Veronica comes home. We both see her through the window, and Leo watches in silence as she unlocks the door. As soon as his mother disappears inside, he gets up and thanks me for the crackers. I walk him to the front door, watching as he pushes his feet into his shoes without untying the laces. Again I happen to think of the note that fell out of his book: *Too ugly to exist.* Maybe, it hits me, he doesn't have very many people to turn to. Maybe that's why he sits here with me, why he oversteps the line of what should be his parents' private lives. Because he's anxious and lost but doesn't have anyone he can talk to about those feelings.

I pick up his backpack and hand it to him.

"Do you have anyone to talk to? A friend or some grown-up you can trust?"

Leo takes the backpack and looks straight at me. There's a moment of silence.

"Thanks for letting me stop by," he says, and then quickly goes on his way.

I return to the kitchen and watch him through the window. I can't help but wonder what awaits him at home. *Veronica.* Who is the woman behind that sophisticated mask? And how is she doing, really?

15

THE HUSBAND

Maladaptive stress reaction.

That's the diagnosis my wife received in connection with what happened to her when she was young. She must have explained to me what it meant, but I remember very little from that part of the conversation. There was so much else that demanded attention, so much to absorb all at once. As far as the medical condition was concerned, I actually only managed to grasp that it consisted of a disproportionately strong reaction—in terms of emotions and behavior—to a specific event.

Finally eight or nine months ago, my wife revealed the whole thing to me, describing her reaction and her actions at that time. She was finally ready to confide in me, she said. She didn't cry as she talked. Her voice was calm and contrasted sharply to the violence contained in her words. I wish I could say that I handled it well. I wish that I could say that what she told me hadn't affected my view of her.

We were lying in bed, and I felt the nausea rising in me. I patted her clumsily on the head and then excused myself, saying that I must have eaten something that wasn't sitting well. I said that she shouldn't move from that spot, that I would be right back and would hold her again. Then I raced to the bathroom and threw up. My legs were shaking, and I couldn't stand up. Every time I tried, I was overcome by dizziness. When I eventually returned to the bedroom, she was lying still, with her eyes closed and her tangled hair spread over the pillow. She had fallen asleep. I'm ashamed to say this, but I was relieved. It meant I wouldn't need to say anything more to her that night. I wouldn't need to collect myself and make assurances and comfort her. I couldn't have pulled that off.

During the weeks and months that followed, she proceeded as if nothing had changed, as if she were the same, as if I were expected to think and believe that. Instead it felt like she had slipped out of my hands or that I had drifted away and was seeing her through new eyes, from a distance. I grew increasingly unsure of who she actually was. Had I ever known?

She had her plans—the plans that had recently been ours together— and she talked about the future more than ever. Every time she did, the ground shook beneath my feet. It wasn't just her that I was unsure of. Who was I, I who had married someone I knew so little about? How could I trust my own judgment again after having so seriously misjudged someone I loved?

Loved? Love?

I don't know, I wanted to scream. *I don't know. I don't know.* What I had taken for granted was gone. There was no longer any fixed point to rely on. I was tossed around, back and forth, and had nothing to hold on to. Nothing and no one. Until Anna captivated me.

Anna. I know what I'm doing with her is wrong. The secret conversations and messages, the clandestine meetings. The trips that are getting longer and longer and more frequent and that are no longer business trips but something else—a flight from home, a chance to meet Anna in a strange city and spend time outside the closed rooms we are usually obliged to remain in.

From the beginning, those moments with Anna gave me space to breathe, a way out of what was squeezing my rib cage and screaming in my ears, but now . . . It can't continue like this. I owe us all the truth. I've decided. I'm going to tell my wife about my confusion and my doubt. I'll be honest about how I've been feeling since her revelation, and I'll tell her about Anna. There quite simply isn't any other alternative. It's make or break.

Tonight.

My heart is pounding, pounding and throbbing. *Tonight's the night.*

16

The night she found out, she'd made his favorite meal and set the table using the best china. She had dressed up even though they were just eating at home. She left her hair down, over her shoulders, because she knew he liked that. Then he came home, helped himself to the lamb and the potato casserole, and said that he appreciated her efforts.

She had time to think that tonight was the turning point. As of right now, everything would be better. There's nothing to worry about, *she* thought. He loves me.

Then the blow came. He told her about the woman he was seeing, the woman he was cheating on her with. Life was dislocated, and she disappeared into herself just as she had done one time before.

Days and nights followed when she didn't get out of bed at all. Dark, pounding hours when she couldn't absorb what had happened. But then, finally, the truth forced its way in under her skin, searing into her flesh. The extent of the betrayal was clear. As were the parallels to the past. Everything was still in her, everything.

But even though he must have realized how much he'd hurt her, he didn't show any remorse, didn't ask for forgiveness.

Sharp thorns penetrated, poking holes into old wounds, and outran something stinky and viscous. A black sludge filled her cells and veins. It took over, became one with her. She didn't feel hatred. She was *hatred.*

Her husband, who said he loved her, who had lulled her into a sense of security and made her deliver herself into his hands. Her husband, who had promised to love her until death do them part.

That husband.

Suddenly she knew, with a conviction that cut through everything else, that whatever happened from now on, under no circumstances could she allow him to keep on living as if nothing had happened.

She couldn't allow him to live at all.

17

ELENA

Since Leo went home, I've felt increasingly wound up. Something is on the move inside me. Some sort of change is either coming or has already occurred. After having wandered around as if in a trance for the last month, empty and indifferent, it's like I'm waking up. Thoughts and feelings that remained at a distance before now rise to the surface and unsettle me. I get nothing done, but the hours somehow pass anyway.

When evening comes, Veronica shows up in the kitchen and starts cooking. For once her hair isn't up in her characteristic high ponytail but is down over her shoulders. She's wearing a dark-red sleeveless dress, and her lips are painted a similar color. She's always elegant, but tonight she appears to have taken it to a new level. I imagine that the Storm family is expecting visitors, but in the end, Philip is the only one who has dinner with Veronica. There's no sign of Leo, but his words still echo in the back of my mind, from his story about the purse being thrown over the bridge railing into the dark eddies below: *There are worse things I could tell you—much worse.*

Veronica opens the oven door and takes out a casserole dish that she places on the table. While Philip helps himself to the food, she pours wine into their glasses. The atmosphere seems romantic—the best possible conditions—and yet something goes wrong. It happens so fast. One moment they're sitting there eating and talking, and the next Veronica bursts into tears. True, I can't see her tears, but there's no mistaking her body language. Her hands alternately wipe her nose and eyes. At first Philip sits perfectly still and stares at his wife. Then he turns his chair toward her and awkwardly puts his arm around her shoulders. She shakes him off, hastily gets up from the table, and runs out of the room. She doesn't come back. Philip is left alone. He sits there twisting his napkin in his hands.

And in the darkness in the house across from theirs, I sit with my light off, a shadow among shadows. What I just witnessed actually wasn't all that surprising, a normal dinner. A normal marital argument. But my sense is otherwise. It feels as if I'm onto something, something unpleasant, something frightening. I blink, and then there's that black fire in Veronica's eyes as she watches Philip walking away, the rage or hatred or whatever it is that he doesn't turn around and discover. Maybe he suspects it, though.

That night I wander between the living room and the kitchen as usual. Strange feelings pulse through my body. The house across from me is dark and silent, and I stare at the façade, try to picture Veronica, Philip, and Leo in their beds. But when I picture the sleeping Veronica before me, she suddenly opens her eyes and stares straight into mine. As I watch, she gets up and slowly walks around the large double bed, a phantom in white. She doesn't make a sound. Philip doesn't hear her footsteps as she approaches.

I take a step forward, want to yell *Watch out,* but no sound comes out of my throat. Instead it's as if my forward motion causes me to be sucked closer, into Veronica, and flung around in what's pulsing and roaring through her veins. Everything that isn't visible from the outside, everything she's holding back, I feel all of it, I'm suddenly privy to it all.

All of a sudden I'm standing in their kitchen. Leo is there with me, and I reach out to run my hand over his hair. It's a motherly gesture, and I realize that I'm his mom. But Leo ducks when I bring my hand over his head, and then I'm myself again. My own childless self. There's a tingling in my fingertips. The tingling becomes an ache, a hopeless longing. *It wasn't meant for you,* a voice says. It's my voice, but the mouth that forms the words is my sister's. Then it's not just the moving lips but also the voice that belongs to my sister. *You know, it is possible to live a happy life without children.* I start crying, and someone reaches out to comfort me. At first I think they're my sister's arms wrapped around my back, then I realize that it's Mama who's here with me. Then I'm crying even more.

My mother embraces me, holds me, is my safe haven. I can't believe it's really her, that she's back with me, so I cautiously disengage and lean back to look at her face. And there she is, my mother, bathed in a weak light, but otherwise the spitting image. She looks like she did long before her illness broke her down, the way she did that time all those years ago when she took my frail, obstinate body into her lap and whispered that I wasn't alone, that everything would be all right, that she would never let me go.

Then I notice the shadow next to us, the shadow of someone twisting away from us, or maybe mostly from me, and I know that it's Papa. I know that he's leaving, even then, and when I turn back to Mama again, she's lying in her bed, sick and gaunt. *Work is the best medicine,* she and my sister say in unison. Then Mama is gone, but someone is still lying in the bed. It's Philip Storm.

He's asleep and doesn't notice Veronica Storm coming closer and closer. She stops by the head of the bed and stares at him. Her face is pale, her mouth a tense line. Then she raises her arm, and something flashes in her hand, something cold and sharp. Kitchen shears? Or a knife? I gasp, and she looks up. Our eyes meet, and she understands that I am there with her. *It's going to happen. Not now, not like this,* I hear her think. *But soon.*

You're not going to be able to stop me.

Her voice is in my throat. Her words come out of my mouth. I realize, too late, that Veronica has led me straight into a trap, that I walked into her darkness with my eyes open. Now she's chained me, snared me, and there's no turning back from here. From here there is only a slow, sucking motion down into the mire. Dark sludge rises around me, getting ready to swallow me, forcing itself into every pore, eventually making it into my mouth and my eyes. I can't breathe anymore. It'll be over soon. Soon it will all be over. If that's what I want.

I wake up because I'm screaming.

18

"I wonder if you could help me with something."

Leo is standing outside my front door, drawing circles on the ground with the tip of one shoe. The morning air is still chilly, and I shiver in my thin clothes. I almost didn't open the door at all, thinking about my puffy face and my bloodshot eyes, but then something came over me: a cold streak of worry. *What if something's happened, if he needs my help?* Where did that worry come from? Was it from something Leo had said the previous day, from what I saw play out in the kitchen between Veronica and Philip, or from my violent nightmare? Maybe a bit of all three.

But Leo seems OK. He looks maybe a little pale and has a hard time getting to the point.

"You did say that . . . Do you remember saying that I could ask you if . . ."

Finally he gets it out, what this is about. They've been given a writing assignment at school. They have to describe a childhood memory as clearly and in as much detail as possible. The contents aren't important. What matters is how well they express themselves. Their language arts teacher wants them to focus on developing the characters. "Use all your senses. Make me feel something and experience the event as if I were there" were the instructions she gave them.

Leo tosses his head and flips his bangs to the side, but a few locks remain stuck at eye level. He brushes them aside and then shakes the rest of his bangs back down over his face. It's not due until next week, but he's already done and would really appreciate my thoughts. If it's not too much trouble, of course.

As I listen, a sequence from last night's disconnected dreams comes back to me. The one where I reached out my hand to run it tenderly and protectively over his hair, as if I were his mother, someone's mother. And then the voice reminding me that wasn't in the cards for me.

Leo heaves off his backpack and pulls out a thin folder, explaining that his essay is inside.

"It's about my mother," he says, holding the folder out to me.

I'm the one who takes it, even though it's not about me. Although I'm very aware of how my hand reaches out, how my fingers close around the folder, I feel strangely separate from my movements.

Leo smiles at me bashfully and at the same time gratefully, reminding me that there's no hurry. I think of the hours that lie ahead of me, all the empty minutes and all the seconds without anything to do, without anything sensible to do at all.

"I'll look at it during the day," I say. "Stop by after school if you want, and we can discuss it."

I intend to go through Leo's essay right away. It's just that after he leaves and I return to the kitchen, the display on my phone shows that I've received a new text message. I read that and then fall onto a chair, trembling. I read those two sentences over and over, and each time I expect the words to transform before my eyes, for the meaning to become something else. But no matter how many times I do, the content of the message remains the same. Thinking about you. Hope you're doing well.

It's from Peter. The man I built a life with. The man I thought would be the father of the children I longed to have. The man I am living apart from. The man I haven't stopped loving.

Thinking about you. Hope you're doing well.

It's only seven words, but between the lines it says something else, something more. This time, this attempt at contact cannot be dismissed as a mistake. Somewhere inside me a silent scream forms, one that wants out but has gotten stuck. A scream of unfulfilled longing, of desire and absence, of grief and broken dreams. *I'm thinking about you, too!* But I can't answer, just can't. I run my hand over the top of my head. And then I keep sitting there.

Many hours later, I slowly walk to the front door again, trying out various excuses in my head, preparing myself to disappoint him. But when I open the door, it doesn't really turn out the way I'd anticipated.

Leo is standing outside, half turned away with one shoulder pulled up toward his ear. He's wearing a gray hoodie with words on it, the same as this morning, but now he has the hood pulled up.

"This is for you," he says.

An instant later, I'm holding a bag. It contains a yellow watering can with flower petals around the end of the spout. I look up questioningly.

"To take care of your new plants," Leo says hoarsely.

"Thank you. That was nice," I respond. "This is really nice, but you shouldn't be giving me presents."

"It's not actually a present, more of a thank-you for . . . reading my essay."

Leo is still turned half away from me, being careful not to let the right side of his neck show. But when he moves, I see them anyway: obvious marks from a felt-tip marker on his skin.

"What do you have here?"

"What?"

I raise my hand and point to his neck.

"Oh, that's nothing."

But he lowers his shoulder somewhat, and when I lean forward to look, he doesn't turn away. It says "Retard" in big green letters, in sharp contrast to the red skin surrounding it. The word covers most of his neck. Leo didn't subject himself to this voluntarily. That much is clear. It must have been multiple people, someone doing the writing and one or two people holding him down.

"Leo—"

"It's just some guys at school who think they're funny. I try to ignore it. It's easiest that way."

I stare at the blotchy skin on his neck and think about the nasty note that fell out of his book the other day. I remember how he asked me not to tell his folks about it and how we then somehow drifted off the topic, moving on to totally different things.

"You should really talk to your parents," I say. "So they can help you. Leo, you need to show them what—"

"Never! My mom can't see this. She's not strong enough."

His voice is quiet, hardly more than a murmur, but neither his tone nor his word choice leaves any room for doubt. He lowers his face so his bangs fall over his forehead.

My mind races, but then I step aside, possibly against my better judgment.

"Come in and wash yourself off."

He has no backpack with him today, but I accept the bag with the watering can and show him the way to the bathroom. Leo closes the door and starts washing himself at the sink. I go into the kitchen and put the watering can on the windowsill. It glows like a yellow sun in the colorless room.

In the bathroom, the water shuts off and then starts running again. I set some milk to warm in a saucepan and measure a few teaspoons of cocoa and sugar into a mug. Hot chocolate was one of my mother's specialties, something she made my sister and me for special breakfasts and holidays when we were kids. Many years later, when the darkness descended over me, my mother started making me hot chocolate again. I remember how she would come to my room with a cup and try to get me to drink. Slowly, patiently. In the beginning, I refused, but she didn't give up.

Finally I gave in and accepted both the drink and her taking care of me. "How could you take it so well?" I asked Mama, much later. "How could you restrain your own feelings and stay calm? How were you able to be there for me so completely, on my terms?" By that point, the disease had already started to eat her up, and she was noticeably weak when she answered. "Angry cursing wouldn't have helped. Compassion is the only way to reach you." Then she smiled at me, the same wry smile my sister has inherited, before adding: "And sugar."

When Leo comes into the kitchen, his neck is scrubbed clean, and only faint remnants of the ink are visible on his blotchy skin. They'll be gone soon, too. What *will* be left is the wound on the inside. I decide to refrain from asking about the who and the why for the time being. If he wants to tell me, he will. Right now, he needs something. A place of refuge, I think, and immediately regret my choice of words, scared of ascribing too much importance to my role in this.

"Do you want a sandwich?" I ask. "Maybe some crackers?"

The folder with his essay is sitting on the kitchen table. While Leo drinks his hot chocolate and eats oat crackers, I tell him the truth: that I haven't had a chance to read it yet. He repeats that there's no hurry, says that he realizes I'm surely busy with work and writing and other things. He actually adds that at the end—"and other things."

Other things? That would be contemplating my ruined marriage, I suppose. *Thinking about you. Hope you're doing well.* The words that have been spinning around inside me all day, standing in the way of what I should've been doing. I had to hold them at a distance for a while, maintain a little space before I knew how I'd respond.

Something yellow catches my attention from the corner of my eye. The watering can. I turn around again and sneak a peek at Leo. Then I pull the folder over and put my hand on it.

"If you want, I can read it now," I say.

"Now?"

I nod.

"Like, right now?"

Leo asks if he can take a little tour of the house while I'm reading, saying that he'll be too nervous otherwise. I give him permission but warn him that there's not much to see.

"The bookshelf is in the living room," I say. "Go see if there's anything you want to borrow."

He goes off, and I open the folder. The cover sheet is completely blank, so it isn't until I turn the page that I see the title in bold dark letters:

"Two Little Lifeless Bodies" by Leo Storm.

19

When I'm done reading, I stuff the pages back into the folder and close it. I need a few minutes to compose myself before I summon Leo back in. Should I treat this like a text, any old text, and evaluate it that way? Is that even possible given the atrocity of the memory it's based on?

Leo comes back into the kitchen, and I can tell he's trying to seem relaxed, but the tense lines around his mouth give him away. He has one of my writing handbooks in his hands, and before he has a chance to ask, I nod and say that's fine, he can borrow it. Then I pull out the chair and tell him to sit down. There's no reason to beat around the bush. I know how vulnerable it makes you feel to sit around waiting to hear what someone thinks about what you've written.

"It's a powerful essay," I say. "Very powerful. I was really moved, to be honest."

Leo's leg can't stay still: His heel bounces up and down on the floor.

"You think I'm selling her out, that I'm making a mistake by writing about her like this?"

"I didn't say that, but if I were your teacher and you turned in this essay, I would certainly wonder . . ."

Leo crosses his legs, right foot on left knee. There's a nervous twitch at the corner of his mouth.

"What would you wonder?"

"I'd wonder how you're doing, how things are going for you, and maybe also . . . how *she's* doing, your mother."

Leo strokes his shin with his palm and avoids eye contact. There's something worrying about the way he's stroking his leg, and I think I'm on thin ice. That however I behave now, no matter what I say or don't say, I'm risking making a mistake.

I glance down at the closed folder. Why did he want me to read this specific essay? Is this a cry for help? Why else would he invite me into his world, unreservedly reveal this kind of thing, the sort of thing one would normally hide?

Leo lifts his hand from his leg and pulls it through his hair.

"Obviously I have other memories, too. Maybe it would have been better if I'd picked a different one, something more cheerful."

Then he starts telling me about a cabin where his family spent whole summers when he was little, a log cabin by a lake surrounded by woods. They swam and played there. His father took him hiking in the woods and taught him how to fish.

As he speaks, the discomfort gradually abates. What he says sets other thoughts in motion, elicits memories from my own childhood. Several summers in a row, my parents rented a cabin by a sandy beach on the other side of the sound. We drove there and Papa sang along to the music on the radio even though he didn't know any of the lyrics. My sister and I laughed at him from the backseat. Mama smiled, and her hair fluttered in the wind as air rushed in through her rolled-down window. The cabin wasn't that big, and my sister and I had to share a room, which neither of us minded. In the evenings, we barbecued and played games, and during the day, we hung out on the beach.

I remember that while my sister was swimming and Mama was lying on a blanket reading, my dad and I built a sandcastle. He was astoundingly good at it, showing me how you did everything from towers and domes to ring walls. When we came back out the next morning, our creations had been destroyed, wiped out by the high tide. We stood there staring, my dad and I, and I remember that I was afraid he would be sad, so I snuck my hand into his and wanted to say something nice. "It doesn't matter, Elena," he'd said. "That's how the world is. Everything goes." It was both beautiful and frightening at the same time, and I squeezed his hand harder. Little did I suspect then that there could be something prescient in his words, an omen that pertained to him, and to our whole family.

"Do you think I should have written about something else instead? Some cheerful memory from the cabin?"

I shake slightly, and the images of my own childhood fade away. I'm back in the kitchen with Leo.

"I don't know," I say, clasping my hands on my lap. "No one else can make that decision—only you. If we even have a choice, those of us who write. Some authors believe the story chooses them and not the other way around."

Leo turns toward the window. His bangs hang down over the side of his face that's turned toward me, and I can't see his eyes.

"But it's not like that for you, is it? You choose what you're going to write, don't you?"

He refers to some article he found online, an interview where I described my writing process: why I write, how I come up with my ideas, and that I usually take inspiration from the things going on around me.

"Wait a minute," I say. "How did you find this article?"

"OK, maybe I googled you a little."

"Googled me?"

"I've never lived next door to a real author before," he says, blushing.

I don't know how to react, neither to the words nor to the hint of admiration in his voice. I feel self-conscious, proud, and embarrassed, so I laugh. It's as if something relaxes inside Leo, because he starts laughing, too.

When he stands up a little while later, I accompany him to the front hall and look on once again while he pushes his feet into his shoes by wiggling his heels back and forth. He pulls his hood up again, and I hand him the folder containing his essay. The laughter we just shared suddenly feels distant.

"Do you have a key today? Or do you think . . . Is your mom home from work?"

He pushes the hair off his forehead.

"My mom didn't go to work today."

"She didn't?"

Leo shakes his head.

"Dad said she wasn't feeling well and called in sick. He didn't want to say any more than that, but I could tell something was up and . . . well, that she doesn't exactly have the flu. It's back."

It? I furrow my brow.

"What? What's back?"

He straightens up and clutches the folder with both hands.

"Right before that incident I wrote about. I mean, right before the part about the rabbits . . ."

As if he needed to remind me, as if the content of his essay weren't already indelibly engraved. I nod.

"The period before that. My mom had been confined to bed for several weeks, kind of barely able to talk to anyone. It was just like that this morning. The bedroom door was ajar, and I saw her through the crack, lying in there with her back to the door. And before I came over here this afternoon, I stopped in at home, just to peek in on her. Either she was asleep and didn't notice that I'd come in or she wasn't up to rolling over. She was still lying in exactly the same position. As if she hadn't moved at all the whole day."

We look at each other. I don't know what to say. There's nothing I *can* say.

Leo shakes his bangs over his face and turns away.

"It's so obvious," he says. "She's on her way into the darkness again."

20

My sister texts me right after Leo has gone home. She texts, and then texts again. I see her name on the display but don't answer, don't even read what she wrote. So she calls instead.

"Are you OK, Elena? Are we OK, you and me, I mean . . ."

She keeps talking, but I only hear isolated words. Her voice sounds like it's coming from far away. Everything about her seems as distant as she did in the dream last night. It's only been a few days since we saw each other, and yet so much has happened. I should tell her about Peter's text. Or that I've started a tentative new writing project. But for some reason, that feels insurmountable.

"Uh, hello?" she says after a while. "You don't even seem like you're listening to what I'm saying. How are you actually doing?"

Leo's parting words a while ago did something to me, caused my thoughts about his essay to start spinning again.

"They bought him rabbits," I mutter. "But then she just—"

"Rabbits? Bought rabbits for whom?"

"For Leo."

I walk closer to the window and stand beside the table.

"What are you talking about? Who's Leo?"

I tell her about the family in the house across from me. Explain that things don't seem right between Philip and Veronica. And that Leo is a good guy, but he's having a hard time. My sister's confused silence switches into a cautiously positive tone.

"So you've met some new people? That's a step in the right direction. And other than that . . . how are you doing otherwise?"

But I can't answer, can only think about the rabbits, about Leo's raw, uncompromising way of describing what happened the summer the Storm family rented an apartment somewhere by the Mediterranean.

On this one occasion, they visited a market, where, to their horror, they saw rabbits crammed into crowded cages. The animals were out in the broiling sun with no access to water. And no one seemed to care about their suffering since they were intended for slaughter. Leo started crying and wasn't able to stop when he saw how they were desperately crawling all over each other inside the cages. He refused to leave, so his parents bought him two of the rabbits, let him bring them back to the apartment and keep them as pets. He loved those rabbits, loved holding their soft little bodies on his lap, and every day he was grateful that his parents had helped him save them from the harsh fate that would have awaited otherwise.

Then their vacation was coming to an end, and it soon would be time to travel back home to Sweden. The rabbits couldn't come. His father was clear about that. Maybe they could give them away to someone else? Or simply set them free? Leo cried and protested, but deep down inside, he started preparing himself to separate from his furry friends. The days passed, and their return home grew closer, but still no concrete decision had been made about the rabbits. And then, on the last morning, it happened.

Leo was awakened by Veronica walking into his room. She lifted the rabbits out of the cage and carried them away. "Mom," he said, "what are you doing?" But she didn't answer, didn't even seem to hear. He tossed his covers aside and ran after her out onto the balcony. It was already too late by the time he got there. He saw his mother fling first one and then the other rabbit way out over the railing. Their bodies sailed through the air in a wide arc before they made a steep dive for the ground four stories below. Leo didn't know, he wrote, if he'd actually heard the smack as the little bodies smashed into the street or if that was a reconstruction after the fact.

Screaming, he rushed back to his room, slammed his door, and buried his head under his pillow. When his mother came to apologize, he would refuse to look at her. He'd scream that he could never, ever forgive her—that he hated her. He longed to focus all his seething rage at her. But she didn't come. No one came.

What happened instead was that his father woke up and found out what had happened. Leo remembered his mother's voice as only a mumble out there while his father's voice grew louder and louder. At first Leo thought his father gave his mother the telling off that he himself wanted to give her, but then he was able to discern the words and he realized that his father didn't care in the least about the rabbits. He was upset for completely different reasons. "What were you thinking, Veronica? You could have injured someone. Don't you get that? A body falling from this kind of height—do you have any idea how heavy it is?"

The last thing Leo remembered before he squeezed the pillow over his head to keep from hearing any more of his father's screaming: "Do you have any idea what you could have just done? You could have killed someone!"

"Elena? Did you say something?" my sister says.

I'm staring at the watering can on the windowsill, my breathing labored.

The purse being flung into the river.

The rabbits being hurled off the balcony.

"How are you doing? You're breathing hard, like you just went for a run or something."

Philip with the red-haired woman. Veronica's tears at dinner the other night. Her dark look as she watched Philip walk away through the yard. And her ferocious scissors attack on that bouquet, as if it were a living body—someone she could picture in front of her, someone she wanted to rip to shreds, to annihilate.

"Hello? Elena!"

My sister raises her voice, forcing her way into the tumult in my head. If she were here, she would take me by the shoulders and shake me, demand an answer. But she isn't here with me. No one is.

"I'm worried about him."

"Worried about whom, the neighbor boy, Leo? Was that his name?"

I don't respond. My eyes go to the second-floor window, the one above the Storm family's kitchen. Even though it's not particularly late, the curtains are already drawn. They may have been that way all day. I pinch one of the ferns on the windowsill, tugging on a leaf. Carefully at first, then more and more roughly.

"You seem really interested in that family, Elena. I just hope you're also taking care of yourself. I mean, I did mention a few things the last time we talked . . . I can imagine that might have shaken you up, and I never meant to . . ."

I let go of the frond as if it had burned me. *The anorexia you suffered from as a teenager. Mama told me.*

"We'll see each other on Friday. We can talk more then. Unless you want me to come over before then, of course. I'd be happy to do that if you want."

"No," I manage to say. "No, no. Friday's great."

I wrap up the conversation and hang up. I stare at those closed curtains on the second floor of the Storms' house until my eyes hurt, then I stare a little more. What actually is going on over there?

I start up my computer and open a browser. The name Veronica Storm produces an astonishing number of hits. The only definitely right one is the home page of some yoga studio a couple of blocks away, where she apparently works, and then a link for a law-student alumni group. So, like her husband, Veronica is a lawyer, but no job at a fancy law firm for her. Instead she ended up working at the front desk in a yoga studio. What's that all about? Because I assume that's not a typical ambition for your average law student. Maybe something happened along the way; maybe Veronica veered too far into the darkness and ran afoul of the law, did something that ruled out admission to the bar once and for all?

There are worse things I could tell you—much worse.

Cold fingers feel their way up my spine, sending a shiver over my skin.

My email is open, and out of the corner of my eye I notice that I have a message. Without thinking, I click over to check it. Only after the message is open do I realize who sent it. My eyes widen and scan past the introductory lines. It says that he knows we decided we'd only get in touch if anything happened. It also says that that's why he's writing, because something actually *has* happened. My heart is racing. There's more—several more paragraphs of text. But I have to read the beginning again, have to prepare myself.

I walk around the kitchen a few times, drink a glass of water. And, as I sit back down in front of my computer, I see Philip come strolling home through the yard. I follow him with my eyes until he disappears into the house across from me. After that I turn my attention back to the screen. I read the rest of the email, and it feels like Peter walked in the door and is standing behind me with his hands on my shoulders. He's waiting to hold me, waiting for me to push back against him and lay my cheek against his chest. *A puzzle with only two pieces.*

I read it again and again.

> The other day I saw a little girl in the park. She didn't want to stop swinging. Her father was tired of it, but she kept shouting that she wanted to go faster, that she wanted to swing higher. You should

have heard her laughing. Oh, how she whooped
when the swing flew forward, up into the air. She
was so much like you, Elena. She had your coloring
and the same dimples in her cheeks, and I couldn't
help but think that she could have been ours. Then
it hit me. What are we doing? What have we done?

I jump out of my chair, ready to throw myself into Peter's arms.
The sense of his presence is so strong. But when I turn around, there
are only twilight shadows in the corner. The room is empty, and I'm
alone—totally, totally alone.

21

THE HUSBAND

She isn't opening the curtains to let in the morning light the way she usually does. She doesn't get up at all. I say her name, but she doesn't answer. When I get out of our bed, she stays put. I do what I need to in the bathroom, then get dressed and go have breakfast. When I return to our bedroom, my wife hasn't moved an inch. She's still lying in exactly the same position with her legs pulled up, huddled with her back toward me.

I say her name from the doorway, but she doesn't respond. I walk closer and say it again. Then I walk right up to her and put my hand on her shoulder, shake her gently and then a little less gently. But she doesn't move. I note that she's breathing, and I see her eyes jerking around inside her closed eyelids, so I know that she's alive. *Alive?* To think that word even pops into my consciousness. Of course she's alive!

I take a step back, thinking back to our conversation at the dinner table, to my confession. Could I have done something differently? Is there a right way, a considerate way, to tell your wife you're seeing another woman? That you're confused and don't know what you want?

In the end, I have to go. Work is waiting. I set out a glass of water for her and squeeze her upper arm under the covers, then I leave her there in the dark. I feel guilt and self-reproach—and relief that I finally told the truth, that I'm not living a lie anymore. But also—maybe most of all—it hurts me to see my wife like this. Yet after all is said and done, tears and apathy are better than the alternative. I think of the scar on her stomach and shudder.

I discovered it the first time we were naked together, but it took a couple of weeks before I asked her about it. She reeled off a story about an accident when she was a kid, something about a barbed-wire fence, and that was the end of it. Maybe I should have smelled a rat even then, asked more questions and scrutinized her face as she explained. But I was in love and saw only what she wanted me to see. I used to kiss that scar when we were in bed together, and now, after the fact, I remember that she always pushed my head away on those occasions. Later on she told me the truth, and now I'll never be able to look at that scar the same way.

When I return home, no one comes to greet me. The lights are off in the front hallway and in the kitchen. My wife is still lying in bed, in the same place and the same position as this morning. The curtains are drawn, and the room is dark and stuffy. I try talking to her, asking her how she's doing and if there's anything I can do, but she's unresponsive.

I neither want to nor dare to intrude. I have no other choice than to be understanding and give her a little time. But at the same time . . . she can't stay in this state for however long she wants. Two or three days max, I think. Then I'll need to do something, bring in outside help. When it's time for bed, I get ready, fold back the covers, and lie down on my side of the mattress. It's an odd sensation, sharing a bed and yet not, being as close as two people can be and at the same time separated by a chasm.

Of course I could sleep by myself in a different room or on the sofa. Isn't that what people do in situations like this? But, no. If there is a template for how spouses should behave when one of them has cheated on the other, it doesn't apply to us. In our case there is no comfort or guidance to be drawn from other people's experiences, no conventional pattern. We're not like other people.

I hear her even breathing and wonder what she's thinking. I realize that I have no idea, that maybe I never had any. I fold my arms under my head and stare at the ceiling. No, we're not like other people, but that is not because of me. We're different because my wife is different.

22

ELENA

Evening turns to night, and I don't even attempt to go to bed. There's no point. I still won't be able to fall asleep. The energy surges around inside me, searching in vain for some release. I move through the house, finally pausing in the doorway to the living room, my eyes scanning the moving boxes stacked along the walls. I ought to unpack at least a couple of them before my sister comes over. That would give me something to do, somewhere to put my hands.

But I'm drawn to the bookshelf instead, where I take out books and assign them new places. This is pretty much automatic now: sort books, sort thoughts. I stretch up onto my tiptoes to reach the top shelf, but books aren't the only thing I'm reaching for. I'm reaching for my mother.

"What should I do?" I whisper to her in the darkness.

If only I could feel her arms around me one more time, feel the calm in her fingertips as they tuck my hair behind my ear. But here I am, sleepless and hopeless and alone with the few (albeit critical) choices that remain.

I've memorized Peter's email and now know every single sentence, each word, by heart. He ended by asking if I would consider meeting.

Without any demands or expectations, just to see each other and talk a little. I miss you so much. Every time I think about those words, it's like being sucked into a whirlpool, as if I'm spinning faster and faster in a spiral of suppressed emotions only to ultimately be tossed back up to the surface. He wants to meet. He misses me. I press my palms against my chest, feeling the warmth spreading into my palms. I think of Peter's tender meditation on the little girl he thought looked like me, the one who could have been ours. And then the desperation that shone through the sentences that followed, the same desperation I myself feel. *What are we doing here? What have we done?*

My hand moves on its own, and before I have a chance to understand what's going on, I've slammed my fist against the wall beside the bookshelf. I back away, staring at my fingers as if they belonged to someone else.

Then I suddenly hear it—my mother's voice.

Work is the best medicine.

And in a flash, I understand what I need to do.

I abandon the books even though I'm only halfway through sorting them. In the kitchen, I start my computer and draft a response to Peter. I write without first reading through his email again, without weighing my words or working through my thoughts. I explain that I can't meet him right now, that there's something I need to finish first. But that then, after a bit of time has passed and what I need to do is finished, maybe we can get together and talk, if he still wants to. As soon as I type that last bit, I hit "Send," not giving myself a chance to reconsider and possibly regret anything. That's how it is now. That's how it has to be.

I open the file with the text I began a few days ago. I started it purely on impulse, without knowing where it would lead. Now I know.

I will finish writing it, combining the fragments into a narrative— yet another one. Because I'm an author and that's what authors do. I will write my way through the darkness, giving this text everything I've got, hoping that when the last chapter is written I can crawl out the other side. Whatever happens after that, whoever I end up being then, remains to be seen.

I can just make out the hazy contours of someone sitting across the kitchen table from me, anxiously bouncing one leg up and down. Leo. I look up, and there's no one there. The chair is empty. I turn my face and look out the window. The house across from me is just a dark silhouette now with no lights on to illuminate the rooms. The only clearly visible thing is me, centered in the bluish glow that emanates from my computer. I scroll down to the last sentence I wrote, and my fingers assume their starting positions on the keyboard. Then I begin.

The words take shape beneath my fingertips, almost on their own. Night races by as page is added to page. When the fatigue gradually starts to whistle through my head, I move to bed, setting my computer on the floor underneath and sleeping for a few hours, a fitful sleep filled with muddled nightmares. In the middle of one particularly violent sequence, I wake up, pick up the computer, and write another few pages before I fall asleep again. This same pattern is repeated until the day dawns and I return to the kitchen table. I eat stale bread with the last remnants from the marmalade container and drink tea, noting in passing that I really do need to go shopping today if I'm going to offer my sister anything sensible for dinner. And then I keep working.

Peter sends a response. Do what feels right to you. Take the time you need. I'm here when you're ready. I read it and keep working.

It's not until late in the afternoon when I see Leo outside that my fingers take a brief break. What should I say to him? How should I explain that today's not a good day? That I'm going to be busy for the foreseeable future? Then I realize that he's not coming over here at all, but rather heading in the opposite direction, home to his place. There's something strange about the way he moves, and when I crane my neck, I see that he's not wearing any shoes. *No shoes?* I stand up halfway from my chair and lean closer to the window. But my eyes are not deceiving me. Leo is wearing only socks as he walks along the flagstone path. *Why . . . How . . . ?* He doesn't look up once, merely stares at the ground. Then he disappears into the house across from me.

My eyes wander from the front door up to the second floor where the curtains are still drawn. As if someone is lying in there, has maybe been lying in there all day. Someone who's heading into the darkness. I turn my eyes back to the screen.

Now write. Just write.

And I do.

23

The cupboard under the sink has started to smell. I tie a knot in the top of the trash bag and head outside to toss it into one of the bins. When I turn around, Leo is standing behind me. Even though he's wearing a baggy shirt and saggy jeans, as usual his lanky body seems thinner than ever.

I look at the time and ask him what he's doing outside so early. School doesn't start now, does it?

Not for another hour, is the answer, but the library is open. He usually goes there to read or study before his first class. It's convenient since there's a separate entrance to the school from there, which means he doesn't have to crowd into the big coatroom inside the main entrance with everyone else.

Crowd? I wonder quietly to myself. *Or risk being teased and pushed around?* I look down at Leo's feet. He's wearing shoes, but they're not his normal white sneakers. I ask what happened to those, and he wonders what I mean.

"Yesterday, Leo. I saw you come home in just your socks."

He tosses his head so his bangs flip off his forehead. The infected pimples on his forehead scream at me—they've either gotten bigger or there are more of them. Then he jerks his head and his hair falls back over his face.

"I have to go now," he says. "See ya."

I get him to look me in the eye.

"What else do they do to you? Aside from sending mean notes, writing on your skin, and taking your shoes?"

Leo turns away. I think that now I've crossed a line. Now he'll leave here and never come back. But he stays put with his back to me. I glance over at the Storm family's kitchen, wonder if Veronica and Philip are maybe sitting in there right now looking out at us, although their view would be blocked by some bushes.

I take a step forward, searching for something wise to say, but it's not easy. Really not easy.

There's something inconsistent about Leo's behavior, something that bewilders me. He doesn't seem to have any problem talking about what happens at home. It's more like he's on the verge of not having any limits when it comes to how much and what he's willing to tell me about his family, especially Veronica. But when it comes to what happens to him a school, the situation is different. Maybe a boy his age finds it harder to talk about things that have to do with his friends, or rather his lack of friends.

"Leo, what can I do?"

He doesn't respond. He shrugs.

Is he crying? It really gets to me, deep down. I take another step forward.

"I really want to help you."

Finally he turns around. He stands there looking at the ground and seems to be debating with himself.

"Maybe you could . . . ," he finally says. "Do you think you could take care of my house key?"

Then he raises his face and looks me in the eye, explaining briefly and quietly that sometimes they take his stuff and hide it. Shoes, keys . . . He takes off his backpack and pulls something out of the outer compartment. A second later, I'm holding a house key. He swings his backpack back on, says that he doesn't need it at school, and that he can just stop by and pick it up when he comes home. He promises not to bother me for long, doesn't actually need to come in at all. And if I'm busy or not home, I can just put the key in a flowerpot or something outside the door.

"That writing handbook I borrowed from you is in my room, by the way, next to the computer, if you need it."

Then he's off. And I'm holding his key, unsure about what I've actually agreed to.

A few hours later, I see Veronica. I'm sitting at my computer writing, pushing back the dark thoughts lurking somewhere in the background by focusing on the text that's taking shape beneath my fingers. When Veronica pops up in her kitchen, it's the first time I've seen her since the dinner that ended in tears. Since then the curtains on the second floor have not opened in the mornings, haven't opened at all.

She's on her way into the darkness again. A hint that she's been through unbalanced periods before. Like when she threw her purse off the bridge. Like the previous incident with the rabbits. The rabbits . . . I feel like I can hear the sound of their skulls smashing against the asphalt and see bloody hunks of fur being torn off and spread across the street. Who does something like that? What kind of person, what kind of mother? I shiver and pull my sweater closer around my body.

Based on what Leo said, I guess I figured it would take another couple of days before Veronica showed herself. Or, if she did, it would be in a bathrobe with shuffling steps. But here she is with her hair up in her typical glossy, well-brushed ponytail. She's wearing a brightly colored form-fitting top and moving energetically around the kitchen. She opens the fridge and stuffs something into her mouth, then fills a water bottle and leaves the room again. I lean forward, trying to keep my eyes on her as she goes around the corner out the door, but she's gone.

It's possible that Veronica is on her way back to the bedroom, that her trip downstairs was all she was up to today, but it's also possible that she's planning to leave the house soon. I feel my pulse speed up and look down at my own body. I'm wearing a cardigan over the tank top I slept in and have pulled on a pair of sweats. Nearly presentable, prepared. My hands are suddenly clammy. *Prepared? For what?* Writing. That's what I'm going to devote myself to now, fully. Nothing will distract me—isn't that what I decided?

The front door of the house across the way opens, and Veronica comes out. She's wearing a thin, snug jacket over her garish top and a pair of black workout leggings underneath. In one hand, she's holding a small black bag with a water bottle sticking out of one of its side pockets. She locks the door and strides boldly out of the yard, the same way her husband usually goes when he leaves the house, the way he went this morning as well.

I hear Leo's voice again. *There are worse things I could tell you—much worse.* A moment later, I find myself in the front hall, rapidly pulling on a pair of running shoes and grabbing a down vest. Then I'm immediately out the door, on Veronica's heels. It's as if an external force has captured me and is leading me along.

I don't understand anything, don't know anything. Only this: I have to see where she's going.

24

When the change came, he didn't notice it. Even though it was like the sky and the sea traded places.

The apathy and hopelessness gave way, leaving room for the fantasies—fantasies of getting even and revenge, of terror-stricken screams and violent death. And then one day when she knew she was home alone, she got out of bed, got dressed, and packed her workout bag.

The day she decided to kill her husband was a Friday. But she didn't know then what form it would take. This was something she would need time to prepare for. Until she had a plan, she would dedicate herself to building up her body. She would become stronger than she'd ever been. There was no assurance that pure raw strength would matter at all when the critical moment arrived, but it wasn't out of the question, either. She needed to be prepared for everything.

He didn't touch her anymore, didn't see her without clothes on, and wouldn't notice the physical change. He wouldn't understand what was happening, and that was the way she wanted it. She would let him believe that she was weak and fragile, that she was still spending the majority of her days lying in bed. She would let him believe she was harmless.

There was a contraction. She felt it in every cell. It wouldn't be long now, not long at all.

25

ELENA

The gym is located at the top of a rectangular brick building. A small corridor with wall-to-wall carpeting leads from the elevator to the reception desk, which consists of a curved counter made of polished wood. A cut-glass chandelier hangs from the ceiling above it.

"What sorts of workouts do you normally do? Have you belonged to a gym before?"

The young woman behind the counter is in her twenties and scrutinizes me with obvious skepticism, seeming to have a hard time accepting me as a potential client. My slovenly appearance is unusual for this type of establishment apparently. I ought to turn around, take the elevator back down, and go home. I know that Veronica is here somewhere beyond the reception desk. That should be enough.

I kept my distance the whole way here, not that it mattered. Veronica walked purposefully down the sidewalk without looking right or left, without noticing me.

When we reached the gym, I waited behind a tree while she disappeared through the glass-enclosed lobby. I didn't rush across the street until the elevator doors closed. Then I watched the red numbers showing the elevator's progress until it stopped on the top floor. On the wall next to the elevator was a list of the businesses and organizations located on each floor: dentists, real estate brokers, a nail salon. And then at the very top, the name of a gym: Exclusive. I should have stopped right there. That should have been enough.

But if something's bugging me and gnawing at me, I just can't drop it. I stand up straighter.

"I don't currently belong to a gym, but I'm interested in joining this one. Do you think I could take a quick tour before I make up my mind?"

Where did those words even come from, and that self-confident, compelling tone? I don't know, but it works. The young woman says OK and gestures for me to follow her. She shows me the locker room first and then escorts me out into the "landscape," as she calls the large workout room. It has a lilac-colored wall at one end and an angled glass roof at the other end; long rows of treadmills and elliptical machines; strength training machines; and, at the far end, free weights. There aren't that many people here working out. The personal trainer explains that there are usually more people here in the evenings and on weekends. I look around and see a couple who are about twenty-five, an older woman, and a handful of men each working out on their own. And then Veronica.

She's standing at the back in front of a mirror, lifting spherical objects with both hands. She's off in her own little world. Concentration and focus are written all over her face, and something else is, too: pain. She's working out so hard that it hurts. I see the muscles bulging and moving beneath the skin on her shoulders and upper arms. I stand motionless, unable to look away from her.

"Those are the kettlebells," the personal trainer tells me, nodding at the spheres Veronica is holding. "They build muscles fast. In just a few weeks, you can increase the strength in your arm muscles by up to—"

"How long has she been working out here?"

The girl looks surprised and maybe something else.

"You mean that woman over there? I don't know. But we can go over there if you'd like. Then you can take a closer look, maybe try to—"

I shake my head, take a step backward. The personal trainer shrugs, says that, at any rate, we've pretty much finished the tour, that there's not much more to see. I'm welcome to sign up for a membership if I want, or I can make an appointment for a free trial workout first if I prefer. We walk back toward the front desk. The girl thanks me for coming in and wishes me the best of luck. I remain there at the counter.

"But she . . . does she come here often? Have you seen her before?"

The personal trainer turns toward me again with a questioning look.

"Who?" she asks, followed by a second of silence. And then, "Are you still talking about the woman with the kettlebells?"

I pull up the zipper on my vest and nod.

"I just want to know what kind of impression she gives you. Does she usually behave oddly in any way? Or does she seem . . . ?"

She studies me thoroughly, no longer any sign of obliging me in her face.

"Even if I wanted to, I can't discuss our clients with you."

"I understand that, but . . ."

There's something in my throat, something that won't go away even after I swallow.

"And even if I could, I wouldn't want to."

She turns to the side and flags the attention of one of her colleagues. I turn around and leave, walking rapidly to the elevator. I don't stop, not even when I think I hear them calling to me. Instead of waiting for the elevator, I duck out the door into the stairwell. I jog down all those flights of stairs. Only after I emerge, huffing and puffing on the street below, right next to the tree I had recently hidden behind, do I look back over my shoulder. No one has followed me. I lean against the rough trunk and press my cold hands into my vest pockets.

I make up my mind to leave several times, and yet I'm still standing there forty minutes later when Veronica comes out, her face rosy and her hair freshly blown dry. She has changed into street clothes, too. I step back behind the tree and blow on the paper cup of hot tea I bought from the little hot dog stand just down the street. Most of the hot dog I bought is in a trash can. The first couple of bites tasted good, but then I heard my sister's voice. *The anorexia you had as a teenager.* The volume was turned up, as if she were screaming the sentence, and I lost my appetite.

I press my back against the tree trunk and slowly count to ten before I peek out again. Instead of going back the same way we came here, Veronica cuts across the parking lot and walks over to the bus stop. Where is she going now? Obviously not home. Almost all of the buses that stop here go downtown. She stops in the bus shelter, sits down on a bench, and takes out her phone. I don't take my eyes off her, and despite the cold having long since penetrated my clothes, I hardly notice it. It only takes a couple of minutes before a bus pulls up and brakes to a stop in front of Veronica. I hear the doors hiss open and can just make out her silhouette through the windshield as she climbs in.

I leap into action and race toward the bus stop, running as fast as my legs can carry me, so my breath comes wheezy and hard. Cold air pours into my chest, and my lungs squeak. I'm getting closer, rushing. Yet another hiss can be heard as the bus's doors close. The driver glances in my direction, and even though he sees me, he pulls away from the stop. Puffing, the bus picks up speed, slowly at first and then faster and faster. I slow down, my legs feeling heavy, and I lean forward with my hands on my knees to catch my breath. My eyes linger on the back end of the bus until it turns a corner and disappears. Only then do I straighten back up again.

If the driver had waited for me, would I have gotten on? And what would I have done then? I stuff my hands into my pants pockets and kick a pebble. Deep in one pocket, my hand bumps into a small, hard object: Leo's house key. I pull it up into the light and look at it gleaming in the palm of my hand. Then I stuff it back down again, turn around, and start walking. It's time to head home.

26

As I approach my neighborhood, a sense of passivity takes over. There's no willpower in my legs. I allow myself to merely move forward, drawn by sheer habit. I'll pass the Storm family's house on the way to my own door, that's all. But then it looms before me, and my legs stop walking. I stare at the pastel-colored façade, into the kitchen I otherwise see only from a distance. It's the middle of the day, and no one is home. Leo is at school, Philip is at work, and Veronica . . . Well, if I'd had the wherewithal to note which bus she had taken, maybe that would have told me something. As it stands, I have no idea. She's not home, at any rate, that's for sure.

Leo's key weighs nothing, but even so I feel its weight in my pants pocket. Then I'm suddenly holding it in my hand again, staring at it. It's like it has sunken into me, hooked itself into my flesh. I take a few steps closer to the door and study the black plaque on the wall next to it. THE STORMS. Did Veronica have this made? I ring the bell, wait a bit, and then ring again. It's inexplicable. I mean, I know that no one's home, but my hands move as if they have a life of their own. There are no audible footsteps on the other side. Nothing happens aside from seconds ticking by.

I happen to think of the old woman who caught me staring at the Storms' house just a few days ago. If she shows up again, if she sees me standing around loitering right outside their door, she's going to be really suspicious. Maybe she'll tell Philip and Veronica. Maybe she'll simply call the police. I cast a quick glance over my shoulder—no one there—before I insert the key into the lock and turn it once. It clicks, and the door slides open. The same flow that was pulling me past this house just a bit ago is now pulling me into it. No intentionality needed. I would have to make an active choice to walk away from here now, and that choice would require effort.

I carefully close the door and stand for a few seconds in the entry-way. This place is extremely tidy. The jackets and coats are hanging in neat rows on hooks; nothing has been tossed on the floor. I take off my shoes and keep my vest on. Immediately to the left of the entryway is the kitchen. I give it a quick glance from the doorway. Everything in there is white, but I already knew that. No mail sorted into untidy stacks, no magnets or notes on the fridge.

When I turn around, I see the little plastic device mounted on the wall inside the front door. Of course the Storm family has an alarm. I should have realized that. I'm ready to hurry back out again when I realize that the little unit isn't blinking or beeping. The alarm doesn't appear to have been triggered. Although I should get out of here. Soon.

The first floor is partly a mirror version of the layout of the town house I'm living in, but larger and with an additional room. The living room is furnished in a minimalist style with nicely plumped-up throw pillows evenly spaced along the large corner sofa. There's an office with a magazine rack, a stacked in tray and shelves filled with law texts, and then something that looks like a guest room. There's a bed in there with a crocheted afghan and a little desk with a computer. There's also an easel and a chest of drawers. There's nothing on the easel, but when I pull out the top drawer of the chest, I find several sketches. They're painted in dark, muted palettes and the motif is the same in all of them: a woman pulling off a man's head.

I'm just about to open the next drawer down when I hear something and stiffen. Somewhere in the house, a phone is ringing. I freeze, listen, and wait until the ringtones fade away, until nothing besides my breathing can be heard. Less than a minute later, I'm back out in the hall, heading for the shoes I'd set on the doormat. But then my hand settles on the railing to the stairs that lead to the second floor, and my body turns a different direction. The bedrooms, the heart of the home, are up there. I remember what Leo had said: *That writing handbook I borrowed from you is in my room, by the way, next to the computer. If you need it.* I feel a sort of relief. I have a reason to be here. Actually the text I'm writing has reached the point where I need to browse through old books to gain inspiration to proceed. I'll retrieve the book Leo borrowed, and then I'll get out of here.

The stairs creak softly beneath me as I slowly make my way upstairs. The bathroom door is open, and I glimpse ocean-pebble tile, a mosaic on the walls, and fluffy towels. On either side of the bathroom are two rooms, both with their doors closed. I press down the handle to one of them, push open the door, and look in.

If the rest of the house is done in a minimalist style and bordering on clinically clean, this is where the chaos has sought refuge. There's not a single clean surface in here, not on the floor, not on the furniture. T-shirts and jeans are strewn all over the unmade bed. There are books lying open all over the floor, evidence that someone got up in the middle of reading, and the desk is completely cluttered with paper and notepads. My writing handbook is on the top of one of the piles. I take a few steps over to it and grab it. *There. Now go. Hurry before anyone comes.*

I back out of Leo's room and close the door behind me. I want to leave everything as it was, don't want to leave any traces. Then I look at the book in my hand. If I take it with me, Leo will know that I was in here. He said it was OK for me to retrieve the book, and practically encouraged me to come get it. And yet the thought of having to explain to him that I . . . why I . . . It gives me a weird feeling. I quickly open the door again and place the book back on top of the same pile where I found it.

Then I go back down the stairs. No, that's not right. I *think* that I go down the stairs. What I actually do is crack open the door to the room across from Leo's. There is a king bed in there with a thick, luxurious bedspread and a curved headboard. I slip into the room, around the bed, and over to the window with the heavy curtains. They're still drawn. The nightstand closest to the window is covered with fashion magazines, but there's also a little box. I try to open it, but it's locked. I move the magazines out of the way and run my hand along the top of the nightstand but don't find a key. My heart is pounding. What does Veronica keep in that box? What is so secret that she needs to lock it up and hide the key?

I put the stack of magazines back, but my hands are trembling so much that several of them fall on the floor. When I bend down to pick them up, I see something gleaming under the bed, a long narrow metal object. *A knife.* The sight of it gives me a thrill, and I am just about to reach for it when I hear the front door open and close downstairs. Someone is inside.

A few seconds of silence follow. I squat behind the bed, frozen in midmotion, shocked by the presence of another person in the house. Is there any way for me to get out of here unnoticed? A series of crazy ideas race through my head: *Hide under the bed, climb out the window.* Cautious steps move across the wood floor down there, stop at the foot of the stairs. I hold my breath. Then I hear a questioning call from below, and I get to my feet. There's only one alternative: to meet face-to-face.

I leave the bedroom, walk slowly to the top of the stairs, and show myself.

"Hi," I say. "I just stopped by to pick up that book you borrowed."

"Hi," Leo says. "That's great."

But he doesn't look me in the eye. His gaze is locked on my hands— my empty hands.

27

THE HUSBAND

I'm at work, but I'm not getting anything done. I sit in meetings but am hardly even aware of what's being said. All I can think about is my wife and what happened this morning. In the afternoon, I shut myself in my office and make it clear that I don't want to be disturbed. Then I stand for a long time, looking out the window, out at the street below my office.

That same morning, I stood at the foot of our bed and looked at the lump under the covers, legs drawn up, back curved, the very same position. And yet, something was different, something about the energy in the room. Suddenly I had the sense that she was about to get up, that maybe she already had. I couldn't decide whether I felt relieved or worried. I cocked my head and studied my wife's motionless body, searching for some kind of sign. Is this how it started that time, too? Did she lie there like this right before? A tight, stifling pressure rose in my chest.

Finally I walked over and sat on the edge of the bed next to her.

"This isn't the same," I said. "Not at all like then."

Her first love had cheated on her and left her for someone else—I haven't left her. I'm wavering, that's true, and I understand that it's enormously painful news to take in, the news that not only have I been with another woman but also that I'm uncertain of whether I want us to stay together. But I'm still here. I haven't moved out of our bedroom or suggested we get a divorce, and I haven't seen Anna since I told my wife about her.

On the spur of the moment, I took her hand in mine.

"You understand that, right? Then was then, and this is now."

Her fingers were ice-cold, and suddenly I didn't know if I was trying to convince myself or her.

I cautiously stroked the back of her hand. Thought about the degradation she'd had to endure back then. How her first love had crushed her completely with his lies and deceit, but also with his patronizing attitude. And what it made her do. How she couldn't handle losing him and how, hurt and desperate, she made up a story about being pregnant in the hope that he would come back. Her plan backfired when the boy didn't question her story and instead spread it around and made jokes at her expense. That was when she got out the kitchen knife.

I turn away from the window and walk over to my desk, pick up my phone, and call home. It rings and rings, but no one picks up. Either she's asleep, or she's not there. But why would my wife do that? Why would she let me believe that she's sacked out in bed and then go somewhere else while I'm away? My thoughts turn back to what happened in the bedroom this morning, and I shiver a little.

I don't want you to hurt yourself again. The thought had dwelled on my tongue but didn't go any further. Because, right then, she moved. She pulled her hand away, and when I turned to face her, she looked me right in the eyes for the first time since the dinner when I'd laid my cards on the table. The look in her eyes was murky and confused. I felt an urge to get up from the edge of the bed, but I didn't.

She slowly rolled over from her side to her back and folded back the covers. Then she started pulling her nightgown up, over her thighs. I misinterpreted her intentions at first. But soon enough I understood that she had something totally different from seduction in mind. She folded up her nightgown to reveal her stomach. Her fingers felt their way over her skin, and even before they reached their goal, I realized they were on their way *there*, to the place in her body where she had once stuck in a knife and cut into her own flesh. One cut, which she had then sewn up herself.

The guy who didn't believe her, who had cheated on her and mocked her, she was going to get back at him. "An abortion," she'd said when showing him the wound on her abdomen. "Now do you believe me?" He did not. "That's not how they do it," he explained before adding: "What kind of monster are you?"

When she told me that the barbed wire was a lie, when she finally revealed the whole truth to me . . . yes, I felt faint. If I hadn't been lying down, I would have fallen over. I couldn't get it into my head that such an act was possible, could hardly imagine what it would take to inflict that kind of injury on yourself. I didn't want to think about it, didn't want to think that this wasn't some stranger we were talking about, some crazy person on the news. I couldn't understand that this was my woman—my very own wife—who had deliberately plunged a knife into her own belly, slicing through skin and fat and muscles, and who then, all by herself, stitched the wound closed.

As if hypnotized, I stared at the exposed scar just above the top of her underwear, which otherwise she usually always kept covered. This time she didn't. This time, she didn't try to hide the scar but instead clenched her fist just above it. Then she slowly unfurled her index finger until it was out straight, and her hand was practically trembling with resolve. She pointed straight at the scar, and when I raised my gaze to her face, I saw intense dark clarity in her eyes.

The confusion that had filled them before now was gone.

28

ELENA

With one tug, I lower the blinds and angle them so that it's impossible to see either in or out. It makes the kitchen feel smaller. Small and confined, but that's how I want it. I don't want to see the house across from me, don't want to think about the look on Leo's face as I walked down his stairs and past him out his front door.

At first I thought I would be able to handle the situation. I felt the words forming in my mouth—lying, adult, explain-things-away sorts of words. But then Leo looked at me, and I was done for. I couldn't get a sound out other than mumbling that I had to go, that I needed to work. That part, at least, is true. The text is waiting, the text I need to finish before I will allow myself to contemplate my future—my and Peter's future.

The computer sits in the kitchen, sleeping and dark but still alive, reminding me that my departure earlier happened so quickly that I didn't have a chance to shut it down properly. When I touch one of the keys, it hums and the screen lights up. For a long time, I stare at the last several lines I wrote, and then I look up. Suddenly I have the feeling that I missed something important, something I overlooked, and that

I really should . . . Then I stop midthought. *Stop now. Stop putting off what needs to be done.*

I fetch a stack of research materials from the living room, books that I have collected and made varying degrees of use of over the years. I used several of them as the basis and inspiration for previous writing projects. I sit down at the kitchen table, making a show of turning my back to the window, and pick up one book at a time. If something catches my eye, I flip through the pages and read a few random paragraphs. My hands are still trembling to start with, but as what I'm reading grabs my attention, I succeed in distancing myself from thoughts of what recently transpired. The stack contains books about psychiatric diagnoses and disorders, about developmental psychology and destructive relationship patterns. There are also quite a few books about grief and loss and death. I feel a pang inside: *Mama.*

I lay book after book aside. The pile gets shorter until I'm holding *Getting Away with Murder.* It came out a few years ago, written by a lawyer who was already bathed in scandals. Published by a small, but reliable, publisher, the book approaches the subject as if consulting or coaching the reader, as if it's targeted at potential murderers. When the book came out, it stirred up a lot of controversy and debate.

With a grimace, I open up the book and read the first few lines: "Every year a number of homicides go undetected by our legal system." Then I turn the page and browse the accounts of actual murder cases. There are shootings, hatchet attacks, fires, fights that got out of control, drug transactions, and simulated suicides. The attorney's own commentary and analyses are interspersed here and there. He's especially interested in what made the cases hard to solve, details that could just as easily have led to the perpetrator going free. Even if no laws were broken, the spirit evident in the title is still present in the text.

My browsing rate slows. My fingers have become wooden and reluctant. I'm having more and more trouble not thinking about what happened a little while ago. *I was inside their house. There was a knife under her bed.* My phone's muffled ringtone brings me to my feet. Where did the sound come from? Then I remember that I had it in the pocket of my vest and hurry out to the front hall. Peter's name rushes into my head. *If it's Peter, then to hell with it all, I'm going to ask him to come over here and never leave me again.* But it's not Peter, it's my sister, and it hits me: Today is Friday. I had completely forgotten that. I step into my shoes as I answer.

"I'm just on my way out to pick up the last few things!"

"Oh, OK then. Well, all right, bye," my sister says on the other end.

I put on my vest and look at the time. Only a few hours until we're getting together.

"Did you want anything in particular? I mean, since you . . . ?"

"Yes," she says, "actually I did . . ." But then she stops. "Is everything OK? You sound a little . . . I don't know."

I stop in midmotion and lean back against the wall. It feels hard and unwelcoming behind my back. The wall would push me away if it could, I'm sure of that. Or maybe sooner just let me fall, which I'm already doing, freely, quickly.

"The neighbors," I hear myself say. "I was over at their place."

"Really? Well, I'll be. When did you get so social?"

I shake my head.

"No, not like that. I mean . . . they weren't . . ."

I try to explain, but the words won't come together; they are tripping all over each other, incoherent. The gaps between the sentences grow until I'm completely silenced.

"Well, whatever," my sister says. "I called to tell you I just spoke to Papa. He called, can you believe it, to say thank you for the birthday card."

I rub my face.

"Something wasn't right over there," I mumble. "She's pretending to be bedridden when in fact she's strong and has plenty of energy."

"Who?"

"Veronica, the woman who lives across from me."

My sister moans faintly.

"OK, but did you hear what I said, that Papa called? He seemed happy about the card, actually really happy. And you know what else? You're not going to believe this. Brace yourself, now. He said that they've discussed coming here this summer. I didn't ask him to stay at my place or anything, but if they stayed at a hotel downtown maybe we could get coffee or something. If you want, of course."

"I have a bad feeling. She's planning something. I'm sure of it. But I don't know when, and I don't know—"

"Elena, enough already!"

My sister's voice is so loud and shrill that I wince. A few seconds of silence pass, and then she comes back.

"Sorry. But it feels like this . . . like your fixation with the neighbors doesn't really seem healthy. It's like you're focusing on them instead of dealing with your own problems."

There's an audible sigh on the other end.

"We really need to talk—you and me—for real."

"OK," I respond. "We can start with you telling me how things are actually going with Walter, between the two of you."

I don't even listen for her answer, just add something about seeing her soon and hang up. Then I open the door to get going, but that doesn't go the way I thought it would.

Someone is standing outside, someone who's holding a writing handbook in his outstretched hand.

"You forgot this," Leo says.

29

I hesitate for a second, then lean forward and take the book I had left on the stack in Leo's room. He thanks me for loaning it to him and turns around to go back home, but I call after him to wait and dig around in my pants pocket.

"And you forgot this."

I hold up his house key. He slowly comes toward me, takes it out of my hand, and stuffs it into his own pocket.

"This isn't a good solution."

I should have said something more, but the words stick in my throat. Leo shrugs.

"Better than losing it." There is a pause, and Leo looks askance at me. "I did get one of my shoes back, anyway."

We look at each other. If only I weren't so ashamed of what I'd done, I would ask. As things stand, though, I can't bring myself to do it. Maybe he senses that. Maybe that's why he finally says it on his own, spontaneously—faltering at first, but then with increasing detail. He explains that it started with notes slid into his books or pockets, and comments on social media: "Beanpole." "Pizza-face retard." "Nerd." "Homo." How that had progressed to pushing and jeers and graffiti on his locker at school, and then more insults: "Gross." "Disgusting." In the last week or so, it had ramped up.

Leo gives me an embarrassed look.

"I try to have faith that it'll all blow over, that they'll get tired of it and stop. I steer clear of them as much as I can, but I'm pretty much everything they hate. I love to read, don't have any muscles, and no . . . girls . . ."

A deep redness rises up his slender neck.

Something is pulsing within me, and my sense of injustice and rage on Leo's behalf takes over and pushes all other emotions aside.

"How long has this been going on? How long has it been like this?"

"Not that long. I had a friend before. Mostly the two of us hung out together, but then he moved over Christmas. And when school started again in January, well . . . yeah."

"We have to do something. This can't continue. I'm going to help you."

Suddenly I'm aware that my hands are clenched into fists, tight fists. Leo notices that, too, and I quickly straighten out my fingers.

"There's nothing you can do," he says, shaking his head.

I don't have a good response to this, so I turn around to lock my front door.

"My mom came home a while ago." I hear him say this behind my back as I'm turning my key. "She didn't say anything, just went straight to her bedroom. Now she's lying in bed again, as if nothing happened."

I slowly turn back around to face him, stuffing my key in my pocket. Leo flings up his hands in puzzlement.

"Where did she go?" he blurts out, crossing his arms. "I don't want . . . I can't handle being at home right now."

I stand completely still. I really need to go grocery shopping before my sister's visit. But how can I turn my back on him after what I've done, after what he's told me? How can I go off and leave him with that look on his face?

"Come on," I say, taking out my key again. "Come in for a bit."

I turn off my computer, open the blinds, and stack the research books back up.

"I won't stay long," Leo says. "I just don't get it."

He stands in the middle of the room with his hands stuffed into the back pockets of his jeans.

"She went out today, downtown or somewhere. How does that fit with lying in bed all the time, with her telling Dad she's sick?"

He glances at me and shakes his head.

"I don't get it," he repeats.

I indicate that he should have a seat, and he sits down in the chair where I was sitting a little while earlier. I take the other seat. My legs are stiff as I cross them and study Leo across the table. Is he planning to comment at all about my having been in his house? When he was standing down there at the bottom of the stairs, surely he must have heard me come out of his parents' bedroom and understood that I had been somewhere I shouldn't have been?

But Leo doesn't say anything. His face doesn't reveal any sign that he holds what happened earlier against me or that he's even aware of it. It's as if the moment we spent standing over there staring at each other— me at the top of his stairs and him at the bottom—never happened.

Leo turns toward the window and sticks a finger into one of the flowerpots, saying that he needs to check if they need watering. I suppose I am one of those people who gets so engrossed in my writing that I overlook everyday tasks. I nod, admitting that he might be onto something there.

"Because you're working on something, aren't you? You're writing something new, right?"

I nod again, and Leo's eyes instantly light up. He asks me to tell him more.

"You don't need to give away the whole plot, but what's happening in the chapter you're working on right now?"

I don't know what comes over me. Normally I don't discuss the content of what I'm writing, not until the manuscript is done. Maybe it's the sight of his sudden burst of enthusiasm that does it. Or maybe it's because I feel like I owe him something.

"It's about a woman," I respond. "She's acting weird, hiding a bunch of things."

"Like what?"

I rest my chin on my hand.

"Well, for example, she does some online searches. She hangs out in certain forums where . . . well, where normal people don't usually go. Violent forums."

"Is that a hard scene to write?"

"Mmm." I brush imaginary crumbs off the tabletop. "What's hard is getting it to feel authentic, real."

Leo leans forward over the table.

"You mean . . . so that it feels like real web searches, ones a real woman would do?"

"More or less, yeah." I look up and our eyes lock. It's time to steer this conversation in another direction. "Hey, by the way, how did it go with your essay? Have you turned it in yet?"

Leo shakes his head, says he needs to revise it one more time before he's satisfied. While he talks, he turns his attention toward the stack of research books beside him and absentmindedly runs his finger over them. Then one of the books catches his eye.

"My mom has this one, too."

He pulls out the book and holds it up for me. It's *Getting Away with Murder*. Even though I was just holding it myself a few minutes ago, it looks different now. In Leo's hands, the cover becomes darker, more sinister. The title roars out its message.

"How long has she had it?"

"Huh?"

"When did she buy it?"

Leo's eyebrows go up. He looks like he's trying to remember.

"I don't know. Maybe . . . it could be, I'm not sure, but . . ."

As he contemplates, he draws out his words. The kitchen clock ticks in the background. It ticks louder and louder with each sentence Leo leaves unfinished, with each guess that he doesn't find the words to express.

"When did she buy it, Leo, when? Was it recently?"

It's not until I notice Leo's upturned face that I realize I've stood up and am standing across from him. There's something about his facial expression . . . My questions concern him, that much is clear. A string of little beads of sweat has formed on his upper lip.

He shrugs. He wishes he knew, but unfortunately . . . Then he puts the book back on the top of the stack and stands up as well.

The atmosphere between us has changed—or am I just imagining that? I follow Leo out into the front hall and ask if his dad is home, too, mostly just to make small talk. He shakes his head, says his father has an important meeting tonight, even though it's Friday.

"But he'll be home anyway, even if he's really late, because tomorrow he and my mom are going to take a little trip together, just the two of them."

"Really? Where to?"

Leo jams his feet into his shoes.

"Dunno. My mom's having a birthday soon, and I guess my dad arranged something just for the two of them. It's going to be a surprise, but I think I know what they're going to do." He pauses briefly before he continues, without my asking. "Dad has been talking about wanting to take Mom hiking in the mountains nearby. He's been wanting to do it for a long time. The view from the top is supposed to be *amazing*."

Leo imitates someone else's voice when he says that last part. I assume he's mimicking his father, but I hardly notice it. My head is spinning. I can't wrap my head around what he's saying.

"But your mom, would she even be up to that? She's on sick leave and not—"

"Oh, that's just during the day. Apparently she's capable of more than one might think."

Leo's voice sounds normal again, and there's a sharp edge to it. He opens the door and hesitates with his hand on the door handle.

"But you're right. If they do actually go on their trip, it'll be kind of a miracle. They've been going through a rough patch lately. I'm sure they think I don't notice, but . . ."

He leaves the sentence unfinished, sneaking a peek at me.

"It's not always that easy, being married, is it?"

I shake my head.

"No, it is not."

Leo says goodbye and wishes me luck with my writing before returning home. But he doesn't make it very far before he stops and turns around. We stand there looking at each other through the last fading rays of daylight.

"I can check her search history if you want."

Before I have a chance to respond, before I even have a chance to process the words, he's turned his back on me again. This time he sets off running.

I stand by my front door and watch him go. I can't move, can hardly breath. What does he mean? Why is he offering to check Veronica's search history? Surely he doesn't think that . . . Something is bugging me in the back of my mind, something we just talked about.

Across the way, he opens the door, then closes it, and I'm still standing here. It's almost sunset and there's a cool breeze, which brings me back to life. I go back inside for my down vest and put it on before locking the door and hurrying off.

Out on the street, I call my sister. I'm planning to ask her what she feels like eating. To tell her I'm looking forward to seeing her tonight. But when she answers, something completely different comes out of my mouth.

"I'm sorry," I say, "but I have to cancel dinner tonight."

30

To kill another human being. How does one do that? She knew nothing of such things. Her fingers trembled as she searched the internet.

She didn't actually expect that death—the violent kind, the kind that involved taking another person's life—could be found just a keystroke away, but it was. Good lord, it was.

She ended up in a shady online forum, scrolling through the discussion threads where people had asked all sorts of questions: "What approach works best?" "What weapon is the most effective?" "How do you avoid leaving any traces?" "What do you do with the body afterward?" You didn't have to wait for the answers. There were real people in there, hidden behind aliases and manipulated profile pictures, providing suggestions and describing in detail how they would do it. Or had done it.

"Don't do it yourself—hire someone."

"Do it yourself—that's the safest way."

"Somewhere outdoors is the best place, in the woods, by the water, a cliff."

"Surprise them, jump out of nowhere, lull them into a sense of security."

"Blunt-force trauma, stabbing, a gun with a silencer."

"Explosions, strangulation, poisoning."

"Make it look like an accident."

"Leave the body at the scene. If you move it, you risk leaving hairs, fingerprints, fibers on the body."

"Never leave the body at the scene."

"Use plastic bags. Wear gloves. Burn your shoes and clothes afterward."

"Bury, burn, dump in the ocean."

Eventually all the letters started swimming together, and her field of vision grew cloudy. She felt groggy and tired, so she shut off her computer and returned to bed. Just before sleep came and carried her away, something flashed before her eyes, something she'd just read, a sentence that stood out from all the other sludge—a tip, the only really sensible one:

Make it look like an accident.

31

ELENA

The building Philip Storm works in is tall. I count twelve stories from my vantage point outside the front door. It contains the offices of a number of different companies. Men and women in serious business attire and equally serious hairdos pass through the front doors. I lean against a column and observe them, looking for someone with dark hair combed back flat. Only a couple of minutes after arriving, I already think I've spotted him twice. Both times I was on my way over to him but stopped myself when I realized my mistake.

What should I say to him when he does turn up? How should I explain who I am and why he needs to listen to my warnings? What exactly am I planning to warn him about?

I should have a plan, think through what I'm actually doing. On some level I understand that, but the throbbing in my head has taken over. My sense of urgency, that something is imminent—something I need to stop—makes it hard for me to complete a full thought.

Finally I can't handle waiting any more. I walk toward the stream of people coming out, walk through the doors and over to the reception desk by the elevators. I say his name in a voice that is a bit too shrill. The receptionist, a woman with her hair up in a tight bun, types something into the computer in front of her and then looks up again.

"Philip Storm left the office over an hour ago."

I stare at her, thinking back to what Leo said, that his father had an important meeting and would be home late.

"That's not possible," I say. "Please check again."

She does. Then at my urging, she even tries calling him.

"Unfortunately," she says shaking her head, "he's turned off his phone."

"But this is important. I need to get in touch with him!"

My voice is bordering on falsetto now. I put my hands on the counter and lean forward. The woman with the bun-shaped face stiffens.

"Please calm down. Mr. Storm will be back in the office Monday morning, and you can simply—"

"If he's not here and not at home, then where is he, hmm? What about that?"

Then I realize that the answer is obvious. I leave the receptionist's counter, and in somewhat jerky steps, I head for the exit. Once back out on the street, I hurry along the sidewalk. *Of course.* I know where he is and who he's with.

I jog past the same restaurants and shops I had passed a few days ago in Philip Storm's tracks. There are more people out and about this time, couples and families and groups of friends. One family is walking toward me side by side, taking up nearly the entire sidewalk. I almost run right into the mother. Without letting go of the baby carriage, she grabs her three- or four-year-old daughter who's walking next to her, and protectively pulls her in closer. We watch each other and—for a fraction of a second—I see something flicker through her eyes, something that cuts right through me. *No,* I want to yell, *I'm not like that, not really.*

I rush on, but something is different. There's a roaring in my ears. *What am I doing here? What am I doing?* It's as if I'm seeing myself from the outside, seeing how I'm acting, with no plan, how I'm not thinking any further ahead than my next step. The look in that young mother's eyes lingers in my mind.

My legs slow down. Soon I'm there, on the street, at the door where I saw Philip Storm with the red-haired woman. What now? I don't have the entry code, but even if I find a way to get into the stairwell, I can't just run around knocking on doors at random. *Or can I?*

I look around, take in my surroundings. Cars and street signs, display windows and restaurants. People. Everywhere there are people talking and laughing and hugging. Something is in the air, something joyful and full of expectation. The weekend is practically here. People are on their way home or off somewhere to unwind and hang out. I look at my own reflection in one of the restaurant windows and discern the contours of a lonely, gloomy figure. Then my eyes change their focus, switching from looking at my own reflection in the window to perceiving what's inside, a restaurant full of happy people sitting together around sturdy tables. Couples, friends, colleagues. And then I focus again on the lonely figure in the reflection—she who is no longer with anyone, she who doesn't have anyone's hand to hold or eat with or hug.

Thinking about you. Hope you're doing well.

What are we doing? What have we done?

Without any demands or expectations, just to see each other and talk a little. I miss you so much.

Suddenly I just want to cry, go back home and shut myself in, lower the blinds and never show myself to the outside world again.

And right then, that's when I discover them.

They're sitting at a table fairly far back in the place, near the bar. They're each holding a beer, and the redhead is drinking from her glass as Philip says something. He's clearly saying something extremely funny, because she gives a start and lifts her glass away from her mouth, sets it down on the table in front of her, and then blossoms into a burst of laughter. It's just the two of them at the table. They're sitting across from

each other with no bodily contact as far as I can see, but they can't take
their eyes off each other.

He's sitting in there, the man who's the reason I'm here at all. The
man who needs to know what I know, needs to have the chance to . . .
My head is spinning, and my mouth is dry. *Where do I start? How should
I phrase this? And, last but not least, how will he react?* The personal
trainer at the gym, the receptionist in the lobby of his office building,
the young mother with the baby carriage I almost ran into, the expressions on their faces flash through my mind. What if Philip Storm looks
at me the same way they all did? What if he turns what I say against me
and accuses me of being mentally ill, maybe something even worse . . .
My pulse picks up, but I think, *One thing at a time,* and the words are
sort of calming, so I repeat them silently to myself: *One thing at a time.*
My indecision abates. I take a few steps to the side, open the door to
the restaurant, and go in.

A skinny man dressed all in black greets me, and I tell him I just
want to have a drink. He directs me to the bar. There are still a few
barstools free. I sit down on the one closest to the table where Philip
and his companion are seated and order glass of white wine. As soon as
I have it in my hand, I turn to face out toward the rest of the restaurant.
I need to see Philip and the redhead together, need to hear what they're
saying to each other. Then I'll figure out what the next step will be. *One
thing at a time.*

I'm close to them, but of course they don't notice me. I'm a stranger,
an anonymous face in the crowd. I'm looking at them in profile. The
redhead is resting her cheek in her hand and smiling at Philip. He leans
in over the table, and I can hear his voice, but the murmur of the other
diners around us makes it impossible for me to make out his words. I
take a few sips of wine and survey the room, trying to blend in while
at the same time contemplating how best to position myself so that I
can hear their conversation. The minutes pass without any good ideas
popping into my head or any suitable opportunity presenting itself.

Finally I stand up with my wineglass in my hand and slowly walk toward their table. I pretend to have eye contact with someone farther back in the restaurant, try to look like I'm heading over there. When I pass behind Philip's back, I perk up my ears and listen attentively.

". . . each drive separately . . . you wait for me . . . and meet there so she won't . . ."

". . . so close now . . . really looking forward to it. The cabin . . . so wonderful."

The words ring in my ears. Then I'm past them and find myself in the middle of the restaurant without anywhere to go. *What do I do now?* I stop and check the time, look around, scanning the room as if I'm looking for someone. Then I walk back over to the bar. The redhead looks up and our eyes meet, just a quick glance. Still I veer quickly off to the side and go around a different table.

The barstool I was just sitting on is taken now, so I lean against the edge of the bar for a while instead, finishing my wine and then ordering another. This time I down half of it in a few gulps. Then I turn around and repeat my same little foray through the restaurant, holding my glass tightly. As I approach their table, the redhead looks up again, and this time her eyes linger on me for a few seconds. I turn away, but when I look back, her eyes are still trained on me. Her attention doesn't return to Philip for what feels like an eternity. My ears are buzzing and everything grows blurry. I can't understand what they're saying to each other as I walk by. I need to establish contact somehow. I need to make him understand!

Yet again I find myself in the middle of the room without anywhere to go, without anyone to latch on to. My body turns of its own accord, my eyes seek out the dark hair on the back of Philip's head and stop there. No matter how I try to make them move on, it's like they're locked on him. There I stand in the middle of the restaurant, among all these seated people, just staring.

They're chatting with each other, leaning so far in over the table that their faces are practically touching. *If he kisses her here, in front of all these people, what do I do then?* Something inside me tightens, harder and harder, while the redhead once again looks up at me. This time her eyes linger even longer. I know that I have to look away, that I need to stop staring, but I can't. An eternity passes, or maybe it's only a second. Then several things happen in rapid succession.

I move forward as Philip gets up and strides away toward the area behind the bar, where the restrooms are located. I increase my pace and approach their table. *You're in danger.* My lips form the words, but his back is to me. He doesn't seem aware of my presence. Someone else is, though. A hand shoots out and unfamiliar fingers circle around my wrist.

"Do you need help with something?"

Philip disappears around the corner, and I turn my eyes to the woman beside me. Her eyes are hazel, and her cheeks rosy. Curly strands of red hair fall from her careless updo. It is as far from a tight, well-brushed, glossy ponytail as you can get. Maybe that's why Philip is attracted to her, because of the contrast to his wife.

We stare at each other for a second, then my eyes roam down to her fingers, which are still gripping my wrist. She's holding on tight. *Let go of me!* The words form, rising up from inside my body, but don't make it out. They stop at the idea stage, stuck in my throat. I gather all the strength I can muster to tug my arm free. I use too much force and tip to the side, losing both my balance and my wineglass, which falls to the floor and shatters.

I look down, glass and wine everywhere. Somewhere, someone screams. I become aware of a harshness in my own throat and realize that's where the scream is coming from. It grows quiet around me, or maybe my ears are plugged up. The redheaded woman is looking at me differently now, her eyes wide, her hands up in the air in front of her, palms up, and her body pressed against her chair back. My eyes slide over to the next table and then the next and the next, flickering around the restaurant. And no matter where I look, I encounter the same raised eyebrows, the same furrowed brows and concerned looks. A crazy woman, that's what they take me for.

From a distance, I see the skinny man dressed in black making a beeline toward me through the crowded room. I cast one last glance down at the redhead. Her lips are moving, but I can't hear her words. Maybe I say something to her, maybe I don't. Then I turn around and dart through the room as quickly as I can, rush to the door, out onto the sidewalk, and hurry down the street without looking where I'm going, rushing across crosswalks and around street corners, through light and through darkness, into nothingness.

Back to the ruins of what was once my life.

32

THE HUSBAND

I met Anna today. Just for once we had decided to meet out somewhere. I don't know if it was that successful. At first everything felt fairly normal. We chatted, and she laughed, but I feel like she changed somehow, that something was weighing on her. We left fairly quickly, opting to go to her place instead and having sex in the unmade bed. But even during that, something felt different, as if both of our minds were somewhere else.

It was the first time we had gotten together since I'd told my wife about us. Anna wanted to know how she had taken it. One thing led to another, and suddenly I was lying there telling her my wife's story. I revealed the fact that she'd been cheated on once before, in her youth, and what that had driven her to do to herself.

Now, after the fact, obviously I realize that I should have checked myself, that I never should have shared that. It's my wife's darkest secret, and I took the liberty of bringing it into the light, a confidence—yet another one—that I've betrayed. No matter how terrible her actions were back then, I had no right to discuss them with someone else.

I think about that now, back home again. My wife and I are lying side by side on our marital mattress, silence like a thick wall between our bodies. Why did I tell Anna about the scar and how it came to be? How could I have betrayed my wife so cruelly?

When I shared that, I hadn't given it much thought. I was mostly focused on Anna. I noticed that she grew quiet and pulled away, but it wasn't until I rolled over and saw how pale she'd become, how all the color had drained from her cheeks, that it occurred to me how hard she was taking the information. And I was reminded of my own reaction when I found out, reminded of how I sat hunched on the toilet seat, sure that I would vomit every last bit of what was inside of me, that I didn't understand how I would ever be able to look my wife in the eyes again.

At her place, Anna was the one averting her gaze from me. She rubbed the edge of the duvet between her fingers.

"A kitchen knife?" she whispered. "Do you really mean a completely normal kitchen knife? Like, she just sort of . . . hacked away at herself with a kitchen knife? And what did she use for stitches? Did she have some kind of medical suture thread? I mean, you don't just take a regular old spool of sewing thread and start . . ."

Her voice faltered, and she grew quiet. I didn't know what to say. I had never asked the kinds of concrete questions Anna was asking now. They'd scarcely even occurred to me. The details weren't what mattered to me. It was inconceivable that anyone could do such a thing to herself, that it was even possible at all. I pointed this out to Anna, realizing my voice sounded a bit tense, maybe even disapproving, but she didn't seem to notice.

"She doesn't seem normal."

"What do you mean?"

Then she picked up the other note in my voice. She put her hand on my chest and looked me in the eyes, very seriously.

"She's capable of anything, your wife."

"Oh, this all happened a long time ago. She was practically a kid still."

"She was twenty-one," Anna said. "That's an adult in my book."

I was forced to break the eye contact. The intimacy was a little too intense. I wanted to believe that what my wife did back then didn't have anything to do with who she was now. I wanted to believe that it could be categorized as youthful folly. I wanted to believe that but didn't succeed. That was the reason we found ourselves here in the first place, Anna and I.

We lay in silence for a bit. Anna had snuggled up to me again, and her skin stuck to mine.

"Should I be worried?" she suddenly asked.

I turned my head and furrowed my brow at her.

"Worried about what?"

"That she'll come look me up?"

"She doesn't know who you are."

Anna rolled over onto her back, taking the hand that had been on my chest with her. That was the wrong answer, apparently. I rolled onto my side, propping myself up on my elbow on the mattress and resting my head in the palm of my hand. There was no mistaking the displeasure in her face.

"She's not out to hurt you."

Anna chewed on her lower lip.

"Or me," I added.

Then she turned to face me again. We looked at each other for a long time. Then she scooted closer and put her arm around me.

"Hold me tight," she whispered.

When I did as she asked, I could feel how she was trembling.

I'm having a hard time falling asleep. There's something weird in the air tonight. As has become the norm for her, my wife is lying still in a fetal position with her back to me. It's impossible to decide whether she's awake.

It can't go on like this, I think to myself. We have to break this deadlock, get out of this situation. I don't know what I want, can't make any guarantees, but we can't go on like this. We need to get away somewhere, need a neutral environment where we can talk through everything together, openly and without any preconceived ideas. We can't do that here at home.

I close my eyes and feel sleep finally coming. *It will work out* runs through my mind. *We will resolve this.* But who is "we"? Is it my wife and me or Anna and me? Before I have a chance to contemplate that any further, I'm asleep.

33

ELENA

Going downtown, waiting outside Philip Storm's office and then asking
for him in the lobby, walking into the restaurant where he was sitting
with the redhead, and walking past their table. *Why did I do all that?* I
wonder. Hardly for the reason I convinced myself of on the way there.
I didn't have to do that, didn't do it for Philip Storm's sake. I did it for
my own sake.

My pulse has finally settled, but it took quite a while. I'm back
home in the kitchen, sitting on my usual chair with my computer
open on the table in front of me. My eyes stray between the screen
and the yard outside. I still feel shaky and off-kilter. It didn't pan
out. I didn't step forward and communicate my misgivings to Philip
Storm. I didn't warn him not to go off alone with his wife. And
maybe that wasn't my intention, either. Maybe deep down inside
I wanted something else. Maybe I just wanted to see him and the
redhead together one more time, confirm that my intuition was correct. The fragments of their conversation that I overheard are still
ringing in my ears.

*. . . each drive separately . . . you wait for me . . . and meet there so
she won't . . .*

. . . so close now . . . really looking forward to it. The cabin . . . so wonderful.

I look at the text I've been working on, on and off for the last week. It's a story about a seemingly happy couple, the kind of couple that from the outside seems to have it all. I write about their love, which she has taken for granted and which he betrays by having sex with another woman. I write about the darkness, which dwells somewhere within her and slowly, increasingly takes over. But is this only my text, letters and sentences, that exist here in my computer, or is there something more? Does it affect other people in any way, determine their actions and fates? No, that's impossible. That's a bizarre thought. But then what's the explanation for the increasingly clear connection between what I'm writing and the family living across from me?

I look up at the Storms' kitchen. The lights are off. That incident with the roses was the starting shot. Veronica's scissors rampage, the way she'd hacked and slashed that beautiful bouquet apart over there, got me to start writing again. *Suddenly she was just holding the scissors in her hand. A moment later, the flowers had been abused and shredded and strewn across the floor.*

Since that night, I've kept working on my text—which was fragmentary to begin with but in the last few days has become more focused—with the ambition of connecting the pieces into one integral, contiguous story, darker than any of my previous manuscripts. After the woman in the story finds out about her husband's infidelity at an intimate dinner for two, at first she becomes paralyzed, but then she decides to take revenge.

Suddenly she knew, with a conviction that cut through everything else, that whatever happened from now on, under no circumstances could she allow him to keep on living as if nothing had happened. She couldn't allow him to live at all.

Despite the intense emotional storms inside her, the woman decides not to behave irrationally or impulsively. She starts working out to strengthen her body and researches how to get away with murder. She's planning something—planning not to leave anything to chance, planning not to get caught.

Make it look like an accident.

Veronica's tears during her dinner with Philip, the drawn curtains upstairs, Leo's words about his mother moving into the darkness again, her secret high-impact workouts at the gym, and the book *Getting Away with Murder*. Everything has its equivalent in my text. The frightening parallels that at first I brushed aside as coincidences have become increasingly difficult to ignore. Something isn't right, or more like: Something is *too* right.

Most unsettling is the slippage in the relationship between cause and effect. It was simple with the roses. I saw something, then I wrote. But after that, something happened. It's like what I write has repercussions in what takes place in the Storm house. As if I know what's going to happen before it actually happens. As if I . . . as if I am influencing the sequence of events. *Influencing or controlling?*

I visualize Philip and the redhead, see their faces close together. I blink and see her kick off her shoes, caress the inside of his thigh with her leg under the table. The images glide together and glide apart, reality blending with imagination. What did I see, again? Actually? I shove the computer away, turn the screen in a new direction, and rub my face. I can't take it anymore, but what can't I take? The thought of what my writing is about to do to the Storm family or my own increasing confusion?

I leave the kitchen and walk into the bathroom. The fluorescent light over the sink hums and a mildew smell rises from the drain in the shower. Or maybe I smell? I stare at my reflection under the sharp light for a long time. *Knock it off. You have to stop twisting what you see, stop looking for explanations and connections that don't exist.* I raise my hand toward the closed bathroom cabinet, and there's a flash before my eyes. I imagine opening it and finding a little note still on the inside of the door. A note that says he's thinking about me, how much I mean to him, that I'm loved.

Like a puzzle with only two pieces.

The thought of Peter cuts right into all the other stuff, cuts through me like a sharp blade. I open the cabinet and reach for the deodorant. There is no note inside. Just like there's no note on the kitchen table when I get home, just like I won't find any note under my pillow when I eventually go to bed.

I spread deodorant under my arms and shut the cabinet again, remaining in front of the mirror. I think about what Peter wrote about the little girl in the park, the one he was so moved by, the one who looked so much like me, the one who could have been ours. Then I think of what he wrote at the beginning of the email, *that something had happened.* Isn't that how he put it? Weren't those his exact words?

I stare at myself in the mirror. My cheeks and my forehead are pale, and my skin looks like creased paper. My bloodshot eyes could probably benefit from drops to erase all traces of sleeplessness and confusion. But the look in them . . . not so easily addressed. There's not a product in the world that will help that.

There's something strange about my pupils. They seem blacker and bigger than usual. *I look like a shark,* I think, one of those shady monsters without eyelids that moves way down deep, hunting unsuspecting prey. I take a step back but can't stop looking into my own eyes.

There's no connection between the Storm family and what I'm writing. My story is my story, nothing else. Philip and Veronica—not my fingers on the keyboard—control what happens between them.

So if something happens to Philip during their hike tomorrow, if he turns his back for a second and gets shoved off a cliff, then you'll be free? Free of responsibility, free of guilt?

There's nothing I can do, nothing at all.

That's not true. There is something you can do. Or rather, allow to be done.

I take another step backward, then stop and think that thought one more time, testing it in all seriousness. Then I nod to myself. OK, then, it's decided. I won't write a line until the Storms, both of them, return safe and sound from tomorrow's excursion.

I won't write a single word. All I'll do is wait, wait until they come home.

Or not.

34

THE HUSBAND

So this is how it's going to end?

I'm teetering on the edge. I turn around and our eyes meet, hers the same ones that once looked into mine at the altar in that picturesque little village church. That day they were filled with tears and emotion then, but now they're black with the hatred of revenge. And I see decisiveness in her face, a purposefulness that hasn't been there for a long time. Only now does it occur to me that what's about to happen is not a coincidence. My wife has been waiting for an opportunity like this. She wants to see me dead.

This whole time I've been worried about her . . . Suddenly I realize that I should have been afraid for myself.

There's so much I could think about, so many images that should flash before my eyes, but all I can picture is the church where we got married.

How did it get to be like this? How did we end up here?

Everything is happening so quickly, and yet this moment lasts for an eternity. She comes closer, right up beside me. She raises one hand, then the other. Soon I'll fall. Soon I'll be dashed to pieces. Soon it will be over.

Three, two, one.

Now.

But wait . . . Instead of giving me the little shove needed to send me tumbling into the abyss, my wife reaches her hand out to me. I take it. I have no choice other than to take it, and her palm is warm against mine as she pulls me close, away from the abyss that had opened up at my feet only a moment ago. I'm not going to fall. I'm safe. My paralysis eases and, panting, I collapse against her.

I become aware of her hand on my shoulder and look up. Her eyes look normal again. Where did the black hatred go? Was it there at all, or did I just imagine it? Could my fear have warped my impression?

"Get up," she says quietly.

My legs are trembling, but I get to my feet, again with the help of her hand and her support. Then I stand close to her, not knowing whether I should take her in my arms or back away.

"What happened back then," she says, "what I did, you know, the scar on my stomach."

I nod and swallow.

"That wasn't all."

I stare at her.

"Not all? What . . . what do you mean?"

She does not break our eye contact. Her gaze doesn't waver.

"There's something I haven't told you."

Then she starts talking.

She talks and talks.

And when she's done, everything has changed. Again.

35

ELENA

They're home.

I see them arrive, crossing the grass as I stand at my kitchen window peering out. Veronica comes first with Philip a few steps behind. My eyes scan from the one to the other, checking their elegant clothes and neatly done hair. No windbreakers, hiking boots, or tidy backpacks, so Philip's surprise seems to have been something other than a hike. They don't seem particularly affectionate with each other, but they're alive, both of them. Regardless of where they've been, regardless of how they spent the day, neither of them killed the other. Of course not. They're very simply not like that. *She* isn't like that. I suppose I knew that, deep down inside.

With my phone in hand, I walk into the living room. I promised myself I wouldn't write until the Storms returned home. Now there's nothing standing in my way of returning to my text, aside from one thing. There's something I need to do first, something I can't get out of. I stand in front of the books for a while and squeeze the edge of the bookshelf, as if it will give me strength. Sadness moves like a big lump within me. But there is something else, too, an emotion with sharper edges.

I enter the number and listen for the ringtone. Peter answers on the second ring.

"Elena," he says, and I'd thought I was prepared, but hearing his voice—hearing him say my name—overwhelms me.

Tears well up in my eyes. Not that I've been unaware of the longing and the emptiness within me, but it's as if it's been hidden behind a transparent veil. Now, as Peter's voice hits me, that veil is pulled away and everything is exposed, naked and unfathomable.

Maybe he understands that I need a moment to collect myself before he asks a few questions, wonders how I'm doing and if I'm coping. I could respond with something every bit as mundane, something about how things are going, that I'm managing. I could ask him about work, about his parents, or if he's run into any of the people we used to call our mutual friends. But I can't get myself to make small talk, not now, not with him.

"There's something . . . there's something I need to ask you, something important."

Peter's voice is tinged with hopefulness. He says that he understands, that he wants to talk, too, that that's why he suggested we meet. He can meet pretty much any time. I can choose—whenever it suits me best. He can make some food at home or we can meet somewhere in the city if I'd prefer. *At home.* Those words stand out from the others, loom up and come toward me. To be able to go home again. But no, I know that won't do. It's much too soon for that.

"I don't mean like that," I mumble. "I can't see you, not yet. I'm in the middle of . . . in the middle of something."

He clears his throat. I mean, I had already explained in my email that I had something I needed to finish before we saw each other. He says that must mean I'm writing. But he knows I don't want to talk about my current projects until they're done, so he won't ask.

Then he goes quiet and waits. My fingers squeeze the phone.

"You wrote that something had happened. And then you told me about the little girl you saw at the park."

Peter hems and haws on the other end. It sounds as if the memory makes him smile.

"Exactly."

"When you wrote that something had happened, was that what you were referring to? That you saw a child at the park, a girl on a swing who looked like me? Is that why you got in touch?"

Was that the only reason? I want to add, but I refrain.

Peter takes a while to answer. I hear a scraping sound as if he's pulling out a chair and sitting down. My legs shaking, I walk into the kitchen and follow suit, sitting down in the same seat where I've spent so much time in recent days and weeks.

"So much has happened, Elena. Enough that I think we should talk face-to-face. We really need to . . ."

His words fade away.

My eyes go out the window and straight across the yard. The kitchen light is off over there. There's no sign of the Storms.

"It's so great to hear your voice. I've . . . I've been missing you. Really missing you."

Peter's voice is closer now, as if he's pressing the phone right to his face. I close my eyes and think yet again about how he used to wrap me in his arms when I was tired or down, how there was a perfect spot for my cheek in the space just above his collarbone. When I had his arms around me, it felt like nothing bad could reach me. I open my eyes again.

"And her?" I say. "How are things with her?"

This time the silence lasts for a long time. Peter hesitates.

"I . . . Not so well."

A shock runs through my body.

"What do you mean?"

I hear him fumbling for words on the other end of the phone, hear him hesitate and start again.

"I understand that you're curious, Elena, but it's hard to talk about this on the phone. I'd rather that we meet, give ourselves time to have a conversation like that."

My fingers gripping the phone are suddenly slippery from sweat. I move the phone to my other hand, try to get my pulse to calm down. My throat feels tight, and I have to force the words out.

"You need to tell me what happened. You need to."

Maybe something in my tone makes it through to him and convinces him.

"OK," he says. "Then I'll just say it."

He sighs into the phone. I remember how his breaths used to feel against my skin, remember the heat and the closeness.

"She died, Elena. She's dead. That's what happened."

Something cold runs through my body and my hand flies up to my mouth. Peter keeps talking, says something that I don't catch. The room is spinning. I can't get a word out. In a parallel world, I ask questions and listen while he tells me how and when and what happened. In a parallel world I come off as interested, considerate, appalled.

She's dead. That's what happened.

I try pulling my sweater tighter around me, but that doesn't help. The cold is coming from within. Short, intermittent thoughts come to me, completely without context. Then I register Peter's voice again. To begin with, it comes from far away. Then I hear it more and more clearly.

"It was an accident, a sheer accident, and I want you to know that I don't . . ."

My body reacts on its own, so fast that I hardly understand what's happening. It's not until I've already hung up on Peter and thrown the phone away from me that I understand. Shivers slowly make their way through each layer of my body until they've taken over completely and my teeth start chattering. *Why did I call? Why, why, why?* I should have realized that it would be like this. On the other side of the questions is neither calmness nor clarity. On the other side, there is only more darkness.

My body starts shaking. I think about what could have been and what will never be, of what I believed and hoped. None of it matters now. I feel that so clearly, that it doesn't matter. Nothing matters. Then my consciousness trails away and my thoughts decrease. I get up and lower the blinds, close the window to the outside world. With my computer under my arm, I leave the kitchen.

I'm going to sit down and write, and this time I'm not going to stop until I'm done. I'm going to write the rest of the story, all the way to the final sentence. And then . . . then I'll . . .

I shuffle out to the front hall and then up the stairs.

One step at a time.

36

She had her chance. In the end, she actually got it. It was as if fate reached out a helping hand. Fate or significantly darker forces. The kind that were brought to life by her fantasies, put in motion during all the hours and days she had dedicated to digging down deep into the dark decay of humanity.

Hatred and desire for revenge. Primitive energies.

The current situation, whatever the cause, had now finally been revealed.

The opportunity.

He was between her and the abyss. Vulnerable, exposed. Everything happened so fast, and yet she experienced it as if time were being stretched, as if every second were being drawn out to its limit.

But then when she saw him so close to the edge, so close to eternity, something totally different from what she'd been counting on ended up happening. Completely different emotions poured in and filled her. It was like she was looking at herself from above, at a distance. Or maybe, she thought later, she was seeing herself through someone else's eyes.

It only lasted a second, but it was enough.

This isn't what you want, this isn't who you are.

37

ELENA

The doorbell breaks the silence. My hands stop moving. I look up and listen. Someone has come to see me. I know who it is, suspect what it's about. The clock chimes again, and I cast a quick glance at the open bedroom door. From where I sit, I can just see the first steps leading down to the front door. I see myself moving the computer aside, getting out of the bed, walking down the stairs, and opening the door. I see it happen, imagine how it will be, but I don't budge. The doorbell goes quiet, and I turn my full attention back to the keyboard.

The hours pass, and I lose track of time. My back and neck start to ache. My wrists hurt, but I don't stop writing. It grows dark in the room, and then it grows light again. I'm still writing. Did I sleep a little? An hour here and there, at most two or three in a row, maybe. But it's as if I don't need sleep anymore, as if I have wrestled with insomnia for so long that, somehow, I've overcome it, liberating myself from one of the most fundamental human needs. As long as I can write, I don't need to sleep. I leave the bedroom only to go to the bathroom or when my stomach screams for something to eat. Apparently some needs are still intact.

I only stay in the kitchen for as long as it takes to make a sandwich, boil an egg, or make tea. The blinds are still drawn, and I leave them like that, but I still make a habit of turning my back to the window. I take great pains to do what needs to be done as quickly as possible. I don't tarry unnecessarily, never sit down at the table either to eat or write. I take my plate or cup and return to the bedroom, eating and drinking while I continue writing.

I write about the woman and the man, about the downfall that must come, about the time after that. And while I write, it gets dark and then light again, maybe once, maybe multiple times. Yes, almost certainly several times.

Now and then, the sound of the doorbell can be heard throughout the house. I don't know how many times it happens, am not sure I even notice them all. There's an on-and-off ringing in my ears. Sometimes the volume increases and exceeds a roar. Usually it goes away if I set down my computer and sleep for a while. The doorbell ringers go away, too. As long as I just don't open the door, they go away on their own sooner or later. I turned off my phone a long time ago. There's only me and the text, the text and me.

The light fades away, and we travel into the darkness together.

38

I wake up and look at the clock. It says it's just after five, and I'm still lying on my back, looking at the ceiling and trying to decide whether it's morning or evening. I can't decide. All I can determine is that it doesn't matter. A dull tone cuts through the silence. There's something familiar about the sound, I think, and I turn my head from one side to the other. The muscles in my neck and shoulders are as tense as springs. Then I hear the sound again and realize that it's the doorbell.

This time the person outside doesn't give up. The doorbell rings multiple times, alternating between short and long chiming. I roll onto my side and feel the bed sag under my weight. The sheet is gray and dirty, and when I look down I see a rust-red spot on the material, the size of a coin. Dried blood on my calf just above my right foot suggests that I scratched the skin there until it bled.

Finally the doorbell stops. I lift my face to listen properly. A strand of saliva remains, running from my chin to the mattress. Then the knocking starts, although "knocking" is the wrong word. "Pounding" is more like it. A series of persistent bangs on the door out there and then, after a while, the doorbell again. I moan and cover my ears, but that doesn't help. I roll out of bed and stagger out of the bedroom, down the stairs, to the door.

"Yeah, yeah, I'm coming."

It isn't until after I've flung the door wide open and am staring into Leo's wide eyes that I realize I should have looked at myself in a mirror on my way here.

"Whoa!" he gasps. And then, "So how are you doing, really?"

I run my tongue over my teeth, feel the residue of a coating there. My scalp itches, and I can't remember the last time I washed my hair. When I cast a quick glance down, I discover the white, sticky splotches on my T-shirt. At some point I must have eaten yogurt or ice cream. I should probably be embarrassed at answering the door in my pajama pants, but the way things stand right now, I'm mostly grateful to be wearing pants at all.

I bring my hand up to my forehead and rub the bridge of my nose. *Say something, then! You see how he's looking at you, right? For crying out loud, say something.*

"I've . . . been a little under the weather."

Leo raises an incredulous eyebrow.

"A little? I haven't seen you for several days, not since before the weekend. You closed your blinds. You haven't opened the door no matter how much I've rung the doorbell. I thought you were dead in there."

Leo stares at me for a bit, as if he's waiting for an apology or an explanation, but when I don't respond, he changes his strategy, seems to decide to pretend like it's nothing, as if everything is normal. He brushes aside his bangs and his eyes wander a little.

"That essay of mine for school, you know, the one you read? There's one thing I wanted to—"

"Leo," I say, my voice sounding harsh. "I look like a wreck and feel even worse. If you would excuse me—"

I reach for the handle, but he puts his hand on the door to block it, preventing me from closing it.

"OK, never mind. That's not why I'm here."

We look each other in the eyes. I wait.

"It's about my mother."

I'm not up to this, can't do it anymore, won't. Even though he's still standing in front of me, it's as if Leo glides farther and farther away, although it's not him who's moving, it's me. I fall back into myself.

"Go home, Leo. Go home to your mother and father. You'd do best to steer clear of me."

Before he has a chance to react, I lift his hand away and quickly shut the door. I lock it, too, to be sure. But he's still out there, yelling through the door.

"She's busy packing some bags, kind of in secret, as if she's thinking of leaving and, like, abandoning us."

I head toward the stairs.

He knocks on the door another few times, but I don't turn back. Is he pulling on the door handle, too, or am I imagining that? The din inside my head is so loud that I can't be sure.

"Go home, Leo," I mutter even though I know he can't hear me.

And then I'm back in my bedroom again. My computer is waiting for me on the bed, silent and terrifyingly irresistible. I get settled, take a few deep breaths, and put my fingers on the keys. And then I write, write about what I've known would happen all along, write the end of the story.

39

She stayed for way too long, but all the same the day finally came when she realized that it was time.

After everything that had happened—everything she had been subjected to, everything that was outside her control—the time had come for her to take destiny into her own hands.

There was someplace she needed to go.

There was someone she needed to visit.

After that everything would be over. Order would be restored. The filth that had been would be erased once and for all.

It would happen soon, very soon.

40

ELENA

Light and dark, dark and light. I turn on the light when I need it and turn it off when it's time to sleep for a few hours. Then I wake up and resume. My back is against the wall, the pillows behind me. My neck is bent over the screen and my fingers curled over the keyboard.

I'm going to pay for this. That thought runs through my foggy consciousness at some point. *I'm going to pay for this with neck and back problems.* But neither pain nor concern for my body will stop me. Nothing can stop me. I need to finish the text. I need to understand both the woman and the man who are part of it. If that's the last thing I do before . . . before that other thing that needs to be done. My fingers slow at the thought—*Yes, there's no other way forward, I see that now*—and then once again they fly across those little black keys.

Then the moment arrives, and I place the final period.

I stare at the screen with dry eyes, having a hard time focusing. I ache all over and am beyond exhausted, but I'm done, finished, through. I roll my numb shoulders in circles and stretch my wrists. Then I glance at the overly cluttered nightstand next to the bed and set my computer on the floor. I have the thought that I need to carry all these cups and plates downstairs, but I'm going to lean back and close my eyes for half a minute first.

The next time I wake up, it's because of rattling against the windowpane. The blinds are down, and at first everything feels groggy and incoherent, but then I remember and sit up straight. *My text, it's done. I pulled it off. I did it.*

I spot the computer on the floor, lean down and pick it up, and scroll through the entire document, trying to muster any form of emotional reaction. But all I feel is a vast emptiness, as if an enormous explosion has occurred, a quake with its epicenter in my chest.

I turn on my phone, whose battery has died and which I haven't bothered to plug in until now, and it immediately chimes—three texts from my sister and just as many voicemails. She goes from sympathy to worry to sarcasm. Am I sick? Or angry? Just how long am I planning to avoid her, anyway? And what about Friday, am I even planning to show up? Or are we meeting at my place this time? It would be nice if I could at least go to the trouble of telling her what the plan is.

I pick at the scab on my calf and fidget. What day is it, actually?

There's a message from Peter, too.

He sounds a little lost, as if he had actually meant to hang up when the voicemail picked up but changed his mind at the last second.

"That didn't go right the other day at all . . . I didn't mean to just throw that out there . . . I understand that you're curious. There's a lot more I should probably say, but since you're not picking up, it'll have to be like this instead . . ."

I finger the phone.

"I see everything so clearly now. Please come home. Let me make you dinner or . . . well, at least agree to meet me for coffee."

Then there's a rustling on the other end, and the quality of Peter's voice changes.

"Elena, what I actually wanted to say is that I love you, always have, always will."

I can almost see him in front of me. His beautiful face with the slightly crooked nose, how the corner of his mouth twitches in that particular way when he has something important to say. Then he's gone, and the message is over. I press the phone to my face.

"I love you, too," I murmur.

Scarcely an hour later, I've taken a shower and located my printer in one of the moving boxes in the living room. I return to the bedroom, dry my hair, and put on clean clothes. It feels like I just shed my skin. In a way that's exactly what I've done, peeled off the old and allowed what was hidden beneath the surface to emerge.

It takes a while to install the printer, but eventually I succeed. I open the file with my text, hit print, and watch while the paper starts feeding into the machine. One by one, the pages land in the tray, warm and upside down. While I wait, I listen to Peter's message again.

Please come home.

I love you, always have, always will.

The printer has stopped, and I squat down, set down my phone, and pick up the stack of printed pages. I sit down on the floor, lean my back against the bed, and start from the beginning. I need to do a read-through, just one, before it's time to proceed.

When I've made it about a third of the way through the text, I become aware of a sound down by the front door. A knock? Maybe. I ignore it and keep reading. After a while, the stairs creak. I don't react now, either. Only when I clearly hear footsteps do I stop reading. They are coming closer. They come through the door and walk across the floor, over to the bed where I'm sitting. They move neither quickly nor slowly, those footsteps. They have an objective, but they're not in a hurry. It could be a frightening experience, someone coming toward me, but it isn't, because I know who it is.

I look up. And there we are face-to-face, yet again, my sister and I.

41

"Hi."

My sister's hair is combed to the sides, and when she tilts her face down toward me, I can see the gray roots along her part. The lines in her face seem deeper than usual. She looks tired, tired and old. This is the first time I've thought that about her.

"Hi. What are you doing here? How did you get in?"

I don't mean to sound disagreeable or impolite. I don't feel that way, not at all actually. Now that my sister is standing here before me, I realize that I've had a hunch that she would show up sooner or later. It was inevitable, downright necessary, that she did. I realize something else, too, that I miss her, that I have missed her for the last twenty years or so. I so wish I could talk to her about it.

She holds a little metal object up in the air in front of her.

"Spare key," she explains.

I nod, assuming she has it from one of her girlfriend's previous trips.

"I got worried. I've tried calling you a bunch of times this week, but it always goes straight to voicemail. I've left you messages, too, and asked you to call me back. I mean, I know how you can be, but I . . ."

My sister's eyes drift over to my phone on the floor and then back to me. I explain that it's been off.

"As I said," she repeats. "I got worried."

Our eyes meet for one second, two seconds. Then she shakes her head and looks around the room.

"My god, this place is like a crypt."

She's wearing a coat and there are little dark spots over her shoulders and breasts. So it must be cold and rainy outside. I had no idea. Not so strange, given that I haven't been out since . . .

"What day is it?"

"Oh my god," my sister says again. "What's really going on here? You keep going on and on about the neighbors. Then you abruptly cancel our dinner. Then you barricade yourself in here and just . . ."

She makes a *tsk, tsk, tsk* sound with her tongue and performs a sweeping gesture around the room. Then she points to the window, looking resigned.

"I mean, take those blinds, for example. When was the last time you opened them, huh? Do you have any idea how it smells in here?"

My sister takes off her coat and folds it. She looks for somewhere to put it and decides on the armchair. After that she walks purposefully over to the window and pulls up the blinds and cracks the window open to air out the room. While she has her back turned, I flip over the stack of papers on my lap so the printed pages end up on the bottom.

"It's Friday," she says, "Friday afternoon, our day. I haven't been able to reach you to decide anything, so I suppose I shouldn't actually have . . ."

She smooths her dress over her butt and looks like she's about to sit down on the bed. Then she changes her mind, walks over to the wall, and leans against it instead.

"But the way things stand right now," she continues, "I felt like I just had to come over here anyway, because . . ."

"Because you were worried. I can tell."

I think that it's sheer luck that I showered and changed my clothes before she came. I probably look tired and pale. My skin hasn't had any contact with fresh air for several days, and I haven't slept a whole night in forever, but that's nothing compared with what I must have looked like a few hours ago.

I'm expecting her to say something quickly and urgently, but my sister is quiet for a long time. When I turn to face her, she's studying her cuticles. She looks sad.

"Sorry," I say. "I shouldn't have treated you like that. And I should have been in touch. It's just that this week . . . it's been . . ."

With her back still against the wall, my sister slides down until she's sitting on the floor.

"It's not just this week," she says. "It's the last several months, the last year."

"I . . . What do you mean?"

She adjusts her position and pulls her legs in toward her body so her knees are pointed at the ceiling.

"To begin with, it's the food. It doesn't seem like you eat anything. I mean, your clothes are practically falling off you. You were already skinny before, but now . . . you must have lost almost twenty pounds."

Fifteen, I think. *Fifteen pounds.*

"It doesn't feel good to barge into your life like this and sort of . . . question things. The last thing I want is for you to feel like you're being monitored, but at the same time, I hope you understand that with your history . . . someone has to say something. It's my responsibility. Who else is going to do it?"

My sister's eyes make the briefest contact with mine, and I feel shooting pains under my skin. There's a buzzing sound over by the window. I can't see from here but assume a fly must have flown in the window by mistake.

"Hey," I say. "I get what you're saying, and it means a lot to me that you care. It really does. But I don't have an eating disorder, I promise."

She looks at me in disbelief, and I fling up my hands.

"You've never heard of people losing their appetite when they're going through a difficult period in their life? That's actually quite common, even, you know?"

"That's just it," she says after a while. "I understand that your separation from Peter has been hard on you. And that it must have been a rough period for the two of you before you decided to live apart. Still, we've hardly talked about how things are going, have we? And is that my fault? Was I not there enough for you early on, not asking the right questions?"

I look down at the stack of paper in my lap. We don't usually talk like this, that's true. I feel unprepared, even though deep down inside I knew that this would happen sooner or later. I think about what my sister had said to me a week ago, before I turned off my phone. *We really need to talk—you and me—for real.* And then I think about my response. How I suspected that something was wrong between her and Walter. I feel flushed.

"I know how much you want to have children," my sister continues. "And of course I understand that it was hard on you that it was taking so long, that nothing came of it in spite of all your hopes. But I never suspected that it was such a big problem that it would result in you guys separating."

I squirm, a gesture that would normally have caused my sister to change topics, but not now. This time she's latched on to something and seems to have decided to follow it to the end.

"I know that I called at some point and asked. I could tell that everything wasn't the way it should be, but you brushed aside all talk of anything personal, and you would start talking about renovations in your stairwell or a deadline or some other irrelevant thing. And then right after that, you suddenly said you guys were separating, just like that."

My sister looks meditative.

"You're keeping me at arm's length, Elena. And I'm letting you do it. Or, I have been letting you up to this point. I thought that if I just waited and was patient, that sooner or later you'd open up to me. And I've been waiting for . . ."

Her voice breaks a little.

"I've been waiting to matter to you."

Her words wash over me like a warm wave. I wish that I had the strength to look her in the eyes, that I could say the same thing, but I can't. The fly keeps bumping into the window behind us. Someone should get up and swat it, but neither of us moves.

Suddenly my sister's hands fly up to cover her face.

"It feels like I've let her down."

Her words are muffled, filtering through her fingers.

"What do you mean? Who did you let down?"

She removes her hands from her face again.

"Just before she . . . before the end. Mama asked me to take care of you."

My cheeks feel tight.

"What?"

My sister studies her fingers. Her voice is quiet now, tense. Just before she died, my mother expressly asked for my sister's help. "Elena is going to need you," she had said. "Promise me that you'll take care of her."

I shake my head, can't believe what I'm hearing. Would Mama have asked my sister to promise something like that, asked her to be responsible for my future well-being, after everything that had happened? When I say that it sounds unfair and not at all like Mama, my sister shrugs.

"You were always her favorite."

I start to protest, but she brushes it off.

"It's fine," she says. "I've come to terms with it. I did that a long time ago, actually. She and I were really very different. You two, on the other hand, shared everything in common having to do with books and reading. But there was something else, too. It was as if there were some invisible bond between the two of you, as if you two knew something that no one else did."

It's grown quiet over at the window now. The fly must have tired itself out. I rock from side to side. Finally I get up. My joints are stiff.

"There's one thing you should know," I say, stretching one leg at a time. "No matter what Mama asked you to do, you're not the one who failed."

My sister watches me in silence.

"I didn't want to be looked after. You said that yourself. I kept you at arm's length. How are you going to help someone who doesn't want to be helped?"

Without waiting for a response, I walk over to the window. The fly is slowly crawling around along the bottom of the window.

"What have you been up to?" my sister says.

I turn around and follow my sister's gaze to the stack of pages in my hand.

"Nothing. Or maybe . . ."

"Did you write something? Is *that* what you've been doing since we last saw each other?"

I wait a few seconds before nodding. My sister's tired face brightens up.

"So you're back at it? Wonderful. That's exactly what you need. I really believe that."

"I . . . it's not really like my other—"

"I'd love to read it," my sister eagerly interrupts, "and tell you what I think, give you feedback like I used to do. You used to say that I had a flair for the dramatic arts."

As she continues speaking, I set my stack of papers down on the armchair, on top of my sister's coat, then open the window wide and help the fly find its way out.

The sky is light gray, and the pavement outside is still wet. The rain has rinsed everything clean. The air pouring into the room is cool and fresh, and I draw it deep into my lungs.

I turn around and look at my sister. *Am I ready? I have to be ready.* And yet at the same time: *Only a little while for this, a little while left with her.*

"Do you . . . want something to eat?"

My sister gives me one of her wry smiles.

"Oh my god," she says. "I thought you'd never ask."

42

"Liquor, we need liquor. What do you have?"

My sister opens the blinds in the kitchen, turns around, and eyes me hopefully. I shake my head, nothing like that here.

"Ugh, it doesn't have to be hard liquor. Wine would be fine, too, or beer, maybe a half-finished bottle? Some old liqueur with only the dregs left? Anything will do."

I laugh.

"Unfortunately, nothing. Nothing at all."

My sister clicks her tongue in disbelief.

"Oh my god, a Friday night without alcohol? What kind of life is that?"

She rifles through the kitchen cabinets, finds a container of coffee, and emits a cry of relief. After having measured coffee grounds into the coffee maker for herself, she puts on tea for me.

It's nice to have her here, nice to watch her move so naturally between the cupboards and household appliances even though this isn't her kitchen. We chat like any old siblings, and I can almost delude myself that everything is fine. I say something that makes my sister laugh. She laughs until she can hardly breathe and has to clutch her stomach. Her breasts rise and fall under her flowery blouse and my eyes get stuck on her hand: *That blouse and that hand.* Time stops. Emotions freeze.

"You're so much like her," I blurt out. "You dress the same way and have the same stubby fingers. Or, I mean . . . she used to . . . the way she looked before . . ."

It takes all my self-control to hold back the tears, but I can't bear the pain in my chest. Just when I think my rib cage is going to cleave me in two or that I'll collapse in a heap on the floor, I feel my sister's arms around me. She leads me to the kitchen table and pushes me down onto a chair, tucks a strand of my hair behind my ear, just like Mama used to do.

She quickly handles the rest, pouring the warm beverages into each of our cups and putting out the last of the oat crackers—Leo's crackers, as I think of them—on a little plate.

"It's not exactly a three-course meal," she says. "But we can be happy there's anything edible at all in this household. Or drinkable."

When she notices that I'm not smiling, she grows serious again, drops down onto the chair across from me, and asks if I'm OK. She reaches for a cracker, and I look out the window.

"Don't you ever think about her?"

"Of course I do."

My sister brings her cup to her mouth and sips her coffee.

"In ten years, I'll be the same age Mama was when she got sick," she adds.

Then we talk about our parents, for real, for the first time in a really long time. About Mama's illness, about Papa's shortcomings, and about the emptiness they both left behind when they disappeared from our lives, each in their own way. My sister tells me about the conversation with Papa again, and this time I listen for real. When she asks what I want to do, if I want to see him when he comes to town this summer, I shrug.

"I feel the same way," she says. "But we don't need to decide now. Let's think about it."

The way she expresses this, how she clearly views it as a mutual decision, touches something in me. Tears burn behind my eyelids. My sister moistens a fingertip and presses it against the tabletop to pick up some cracker crumbs.

"When Papa met whatever-her-name-is and moved away," she says, "was that even half a year after Mama died? That was lame, actually. I remember that all I could think was that I would never be included again. I think that's when I decided I would never have kids, ever."

"And for me, it was the same thing, only the opposite," I say. "That was when I started longing to form my own family."

"That's why it was such a hard blow for you when you couldn't get pregnant," my sister says with a nod. "How long had you and Peter been trying when—"

"A long time." My eyes are drawn to the window, to Leo's yellow watering can. "I so wanted to be someone's mother."

She leans forward and pats my hand.

"I know," she says. "I know."

A movement behind a bush out in the yard catches my attention, and I see Veronica walking along. She's carrying two pieces of luggage, a larger brown case made of leather and a slightly smaller bag made of black fabric. They both look quite full. There is something jerky about her movements, and her footsteps seem determined. A gray SUV is parked at the curb with the back facing this way, and she opens its trunk and tosses in both of the bags.

"So you're working again. I mean, that's fantastic, right? Won't you tell me what you're working on?"

Veronica closes the trunk and walks back to the house. I exhale the breath that had seemed frozen in my chest and turn toward my sister. She has an encouraging look on her face, and I realize that her words are an attempt to turn my thoughts away from everything having to do with grief and longing and deceit. I look her in the eye, and something slowly builds up inside me, something that billows back and forth. *Can't say anything. Must say something. Say something, anything.*

"I'm finished, actually."

My sister, who was reaching for another cracker, stops short and stares at me.

"Finished? You're kidding me, right?"

I cup my hands around my teacup and look down at the table. "No, I'm not kidding."

"But my god, woman! You wrote a whole book in . . . what, a couple of weeks? Is that even possible?"

Before I have a chance to respond, I see Veronica return. This time she's jogging across the yard. Her face is contorted. Is she crying? Or is she angry? It only takes her a few seconds to get from the house to the car. She jumps in and drives away. The gravel sprays from under the tires as the SUV disappears. I force myself to look away, force myself to focus on what's important and real, what I can effect, what I need to deal with.

I turn to my sister, away from the window. She wants to talk more about my manuscript. She's bubbling with questions. I finally manage to stop her.

"I have something to say."

"Yes?"

I run my fingertip along the rim of my half-full teacup.

"I . . . Peter got in touch."

"What? When?"

"Several times, actually."

"I thought you guys had decided not to have any contact at all for three months?"

"Yeah."

"Well, what did he want?"

I feel her curious eyes on me and finger the handle of my cup. I don't know why I started from this end or how to proceed from here. When I open my mouth again, my voice is rough.

"He . . . There was an accident. That's what he said."

"An accident? Elena, what are you talking about? What kind of—"

My sister stops talking so abruptly that I have to look up. Her eyes have moved from me and are now pointed straight out the window.

"Who's that out there?"

I've been sitting with my back to the window, but when I turn around to see what she's looking at, I know even before I see him: *Leo*. He's pounding on my front door. A second later, I know: *This is for real.*

I leap up and hurry to the door. The lock sticks, and I tug at the handle. It feels like it takes forever before I finally get the door open. Leo starts talking—yelling—before the door is even fully open. I step out of the house and close the door behind me so my sister doesn't hear.

"My mother's gone. She left! It's just like I said, isn't it? I just had a feeling!"

His face is pale, and the skin under his eyes bears traces of bluish-black circles. It's odd to describe a boy his age with words like "haggard," and yet that's what comes to mind. He's haggard and hysterical. It would be easy to get caught up in his emotional storm. I'm on edge myself. Only take a little shove, and I'd fall.

"Please, Elena, you have to help me. I don't know what to do. There isn't anyone else. I don't have anyone else to . . ."

He clasps his hands in front of his body, and something grows quiet within me, quiet and calm.

"Leo," I say. "Of course, I'll help you. Try to calm down now and tell me what happened."

He's been lying awake the last few nights, listening in the darkness, he explains quickly. He figured his mother would choose to sneak out and disappear when everyone was asleep. He's really tried to keep track of her, but when it happened, he still wasn't prepared. He came home, just now, and found this note on the kitchen table.

He hands me a wrinkled piece of paper.

I love you, Leo. Never forget it. Mama

Leo is shifting his weight from one foot to the other.

"I don't know where she went," he wails. "I don't know where she is!"

"Have you tried calling her?"

"Her phone is off."

I so want to say something reassuring, tell him that Veronica's surely just running an errand and will be back soon. But I watched her toss those bags in the car, saw the look on her face.

"Your father," I say instead. "Have you talked to him? Maybe he knows."

Leo looks to the side, in through my kitchen window. Presumably he's already seen my sister in there and realizes that she can hear what we're saying, but he's too upset to let that stop him.

"There's no point. He's not home. They had a huge fight last night. I heard something about the cabin. It sounded like my dad was planning to spend the weekend up there. My mom got angry and screamed at him. I couldn't hear what she said. I was covering my ears. And now . . . I guess he already went?"

Something pops into my mind: that conversation between Philip and the redhead at the restaurant.

. . . each drive separately . . . you wait for me . . . and meet there so she won't . . .

. . . so close now . . . really looking forward to it. The cabin . . . so wonderful.

The blood drains out of my face. Maybe Leo can tell that something has occurred to me, because he takes an anxious step closer.

"My mom isn't doing very well. I know that. But you don't think she's planning to . . ."

When I don't respond right away, he takes yet another step closer and tugs on my arm.

"No! Tell me she's not planning to . . . !"

With great effort, I pull myself together.

"No, Leo," I say as calmly as I can. "Your mom's not planning to kill herself. She wouldn't have needed to pack anything if she was, right? I saw her leave, and she had luggage with her."

As if she were planning to disappear, I suddenly thought, *do what she had to do and then get away, leave everything behind.*

Leo becomes agitated and wants to know exactly what I saw and how his mom seemed, but I no longer hear what he's saying.

Suddenly I realize what I need to do, what's needed from me. Deep down inside I am simultaneously burning hot and freezing cold.

"Your summer place," I hear myself say. "Where is it?"

Leo stops short and looks at me blankly.

"Do you want me to help you? If so, then you need to trust me. I need the address of your cabin. Right now."

Leo pulls his phone out of his pocket and maps the directions. I tell him to send me the link and turn around and yell to my sister. It turns out she's already standing right behind me. She looks both bewildered and annoyed.

"What is this all about, Elena? What's going on?"

"How did you get over here? Did you drive or take the bus?"

My sister says she drove. Her car is parked just around the corner.

"Can I borrow your keys?"

"I don't understand. What are you going to do?"

I pull on my vest and then hold my hand out to her urgently.

"Please? I'll explain later. Trust me for now."

Yet another person I'm asking to place their trust in me even though I don't deserve it. I try not to think about all the things I owe people and my shortfalls, try to focus on the fact that I'm doing the right thing. For once. Finally.

The look on my sister's face changes. Without further ado, she reaches for her purse, takes out her car key, and presses the key and my phone into my hand. I stuff the phone into my vest pocket and wrap my fingers around the key and squeeze.

"Thank you."

Our eyes meet. *So much left to do.* It feels hot behind my eyes.

"Will you wait here?" I ask. "Until I get back?"

My sister gives me one of her wry smiles and says she has no intention of leaving until I've brought her car back. Then she grows serious again and quickly strokes my cheek.

"Be careful," she mumbles. "I only have one sister."

I start to head toward my sister's car, but Leo moves to stand in my way.

"I'm coming with you," he says.

I look into his worried eyes and think about the violent conclusion to the story I just wrote. I picture Veronica rushing into the summer cabin, crazed with her desire for revenge, and how the world becomes streaked red with blood. Scenes that no child should have to witness.

"It's better that you stay here," I say as calmly as I can.

"But I—"

"In case she comes back. You never know."

Leo stares at me. I hold my breath and try to look like I believe what I just said might actually be plausible.

"OK," he finally agrees.

"I'll be in touch," I say. "As soon as I can."

Leo responds with silence, his eyes two bottomless wells in his pale face. I feel a sting inside. I realize I may not have another chance. Anything that needs to be said should be said now.

"Hey, I'm sorry about what happened the other day. When you came over and I shut the door in your face. You didn't do anything wrong. It didn't have anything to do with you. I'm the one who—"

"It's OK."

I shake my head.

"No, it wasn't OK of me to do that. I want you to know that, that it wasn't OK at all. I'm glad you were brave enough to try again."

Then I walk away with long but controlled steps. I don't turn around a single time, don't know if they're still standing there watching me. For safety's sake, I wait until I'm around the corner and out of sight before I break into a run. I see my sister's car and pick up the pace a bit. Only now do I allow myself to relax, to feel the terror.

Oh, Veronica, what are you planning to do?

I throw myself into the driver's seat and turn the key. Then I floor it, following in Veronica's footsteps. Toward doom.

43

Fast, bordering on reckless, that's how I drive. But it's late Friday afternoon, and it takes time to get out of town. In some spots, traffic is so heavy and slow that I start yelling. At one point, I have to stop myself from jumping out of the car and continuing by foot. Adrenaline bolts through my body. How much of a head start does Veronica have? Fifteen minutes? More? *She's probably stuck in traffic, too, right?* I cling to that thought, needing to believe it's true, because then I can hopefully catch up to her as soon as we're out of the city.

But as the height of the buildings along the side of the road gets shorter and the traffic lights fewer and farther between and traffic thins out, what can't happen does. I take a wrong turn. Realizing that I turned left too soon, I swear out loud and hit the steering wheel. I slow down and do a U-turn, turning right across the solid line, and I don't care about my fellow motorists' angry honks. All I can think about is that I'm losing valuable minutes. My head is throbbing. *Fuck, fuck, fuck.* Then I'm back on the right road and I floor it. I pass one car, then another. The sun sinks toward the horizon. No sign of a gray SUV yet.

I picture Philip, unlocking and opening the door to the cabin, the cabin he, Veronica, and Leo have been to so many times, where they spend their weekends and celebrated holidays, laughing and resting and spending time together, just the three of them. Now he brings a stranger over the threshold. He lets her tromp right into their most sacred space—and trample it. He crosses the limit of decency so uncaringly, so unsuspectingly. And he underestimates his wife, underestimates the strength of her anger, the unbridled power of her desire for revenge. What will Veronica do when she gets there? What is she planning? Lines of text flicker past—sentences I wrote during the last week.

The intensity in the air between them one second and then, a moment later, stillness and silence, deadly silence.

My fingers tighten around the steering wheel.

The life and bustle of the city feels increasingly distant. The highway stretches out ahead of the windshield without much variation. The exits are few and far between. The longer I travel, the more bucolic it becomes. After a while, a gas station appears on the right-hand side, and as I approach, another car pulls out of it—a gray SUV. The driver zooms past, and I catch a blurry profile, but there's no doubt: *It's Veronica!* She must have stopped to fill up, maybe buy something.

I slow down and settle in at a comfortable distance behind the car with Veronica's nervous facial expressions and jerky movements fresh in my mind, remembering how the gravel sprayed from under her tires when she pulled away. But there's no sign of her agitated mental state here on the highway. The SUV doesn't weave in the lane. It just proceeds calmly and soberly ahead. No reckless passing, no furious speed. Quite the contrary, Veronica sticks to the speed limit and doesn't seem to be in a hurry. But maybe she's taking her time for a reason. Maybe she's waiting for it to get dark out.

We continue for another fifteen or twenty minutes before she signals and takes an exit that leads to a traffic circle and then onto a narrower country road. There's one car between us. A small bridge leads over a stream, and we pass a farm with brown-speckled cows in a pasture. Then the woods take over altogether. We drive for a long time without anything other than conifers visible on either side of the roadway. The sun peeks between the trunks every now and then, its light richer and now flame colored.

After a while, the driver ahead of me turns off onto a side street, and there's no longer anything between me and the SUV's taillights. There are no other cars in sight, neither farther ahead nor behind me. The woods grow ever denser. Finally the SUV signals again and turns onto a road leading into the thick of the woods, a road so narrow that I probably would have missed it otherwise.

The road is rough and uneven. The car bumps, and I drive even slower. The sun has set, and it's dark in among the tree trunks. Way up ahead I see the glow from the SUV's lights. There are a few cabins along the road, but we pass them, penetrating deeper into the woods. My heart is pounding harder and harder in my chest. We must be almost there. What will happen then?

The SUV is no more than maybe fifty yards ahead of me now and veers left at a fork in the road. A few seconds later, I do the same. We pass several cabins of various sizes, and then the woods thin out a tiny bit. There's something reflective a little farther ahead, and I realize it must be the lake where they used to go swimming and fishing when Leo was little. Just then the gray vehicle slows down and parks, and oddly enough only then do I notice it: the Storm family's cabin. It's right at the edge of the forest and looks exactly like I'd imagined after hearing Leo's description. A wooden gable facing the narrow road, a patio, and a balcony. The front door isn't visible from here. It must be on the other side, facing the water.

I scan the patio with the covered grill and the stacked furniture, then the balcony with its empty window boxes on the upper floor. All the windows are dark. That doesn't seem right to me. *This isn't how it's supposed to be.* As if in a trance, I open my car door and get out. The SUV's lights are off now, and it's too dark to determine if Veronica is still in the car. I think I hear the sound of footsteps hurrying across the gravel, but then the noise is swallowed by the soft grass and can no longer be heard.

"Hello!" I yell into the darkness.

No response.

Something is wrong. Something is very, very wrong. *Get back in the car and drive away,* a voice whispers inside me. Instead, as quietly as I can, I sneak closer to the cabin. *It's over,* the voice continues, *don't you understand that? It's over. Go!* But I can't. I have to finish what I'm doing. For Leo's sake, and for my own.

Slowly and cautiously, so I won't trip over a root or a stump, I make my way forward. The cabin and the gray SUV, which is parked right by the cabin, are the only things whose outlines can be discerned. Everything else is distorted by shadows. How did it get so dark so quickly? I take another few steps, then look up and focus on the house. There are two windows on this side, but no lights on inside as far as I can tell. The windowpanes stare back at me like a couple of empty eye sockets.

From somewhere I hear a quiet crunch and then the sound of a branch breaking. For several seconds, I stand still, listening to the woods. Then I continue sneaking closer. The SUV sits silently, but is it empty, or is someone sitting inside of it? I imagine someone is but can't be sure. It could just as easily be the seat and the headrest that make it look like someone is in there, leaning back. Leaning back or dead.

Soft grass beneath my feet, the cool evening breeze on my face. Soon I'm up next to the SUV. Only a few more steps and I can look right into the vehicle. Instinctively I clench my fists and stare through the window. There's no one inside.

As I turn around again, I see her come running from the other direction, heading for the cabin. Despite the darkness, there's no doubt that the figure racing across the lawn is Veronica. The high ponytail whips back and forth across her back, and she's holding something in her hand. I can't see what it is, but suddenly I know—*the knife*, the one that was under her bed! The pieces begin to come together, and in a fraction of a second, I understand exactly what's happening.

Philip and the redhead must have parked on the other side of the cabin, closer to the front door. They probably had heavy grocery bags with them, meals that they intended to cook together, but then they walked in the door and lust took over. Maybe they tumbled into bed without worrying about turning on any of the lights. Maybe they're having sex right now. In a few seconds, Veronica will fling open the door and surprise them at their most vulnerable.

Yet another passage of text flickers through my mind, and my body stiffens.

Did she already know how it was going to end when she went there, that the other woman, the lover, wouldn't survive this encounter between them?

I hurry forward, running as fast as I can. I need to catch up to Veronica before she reaches the cabin, before she yanks open the door and storms in. I have to keep her from spreading blood and destruction around her, from ruining her own life and those of the people she loves. She turns her head slightly and sees me coming. She has a head start, but I'm not far behind. When she picks up her pace, I do, too. My consciousness shrinks, reduced to a few sensory impressions. There's a metallic taste in my mouth, the sound of nearby footsteps when the lawn switches to gravel, a wooden front porch with substantial railings all the way around. Only a few steps left now, then I've caught up.

A solitary round porch light illuminates the wooden deck and throws a spooky gleam over Veronica, who has reached the door. She fumbles with something, drops what she's holding, and turns around. Her face is pale and contorted. A scream finds its way up and out of her throat, sounding almost like an animal's cry, and I slow, stopping right in front of her.

"Veronica," I pant, "you can't—"

I don't have a chance to say any more before she lunges. An instant later something smacks my rib cage and I lose my balance, teetering to the side and colliding with the railing. There's a loud crunch above and behind my eyes, then everything goes quiet, so quiet. I fall down and lie there. Something warm and sticky flows over my face, over my neck—and when I look up, Veronica is standing over me.

Then I can't see anything, because the warm redness is everywhere now, blinding me.

Then it's not red anymore, but black.

And after the black . . . after the black, I see only white.

I sink down, rise up.

Mama, are you there?

44

She's in her sickbed, propped up on the pillows I stuffed behind her back, and her whole body is in pain. The medicine she takes now isn't real medicine, not anymore. That phase is over. Now she just takes pills for pain relief, to take the edge off. None of us knows how much it's helping. Papa has grown hard-set, hardly says anything at all. Sometimes it feels like he's somewhere else, even though I hear him banging around in the kitchen. My sister came home from London after the doctor advised us to gather the family. Mama never complains, but I see her grimacing when she can't stop herself. It gets me every time. We don't talk about it, but we both know it. My father and sister know it, too, of course. There's not much time left now.

Mama reaches for me, indicating that she wants me close. Her body is emaciated. Her face is like a mask, stretched over her skull. I carefully get onto her bed and crawl over next to her, cautiously so that I don't put too much weight on her or hold her too hard. Soon I'll never have another chance to hug her. Even though I try to stop them, the tears well up in my eyes. Mama pats my hand.

"You miss me already?"

I don't want to cry, don't want to make it harder for her, but it's too late. The tears are pouring down my cheeks now. All I can do is nod.

"You know that I'll always be with you."

I understand that Mama means well, and yet something within me resists.

"Don't say that," I mumble. "Don't say that, because it's not true."

"But it is true, Elena. It's not mumbo jumbo. It's not about beliefs or religion. It's about us and all the things that connect us. I'm in your thoughts, whenever you want, for as long as you want. As long as you remember me, I'll exist."

The dream is a memory, one of the last I have of Mama, and when I wake up my cheeks are wet from tears. I bring my hand up to wipe away the tears, but instead there are red, sticky streaks on my fingers. It's not tears, but blood that's running down into my eyes. Then I spot Veronica. She's standing over me, and immediately everything comes back. This isn't a dream. I'm not sleeping. I'm . . . She's—

No! The scream forms deep within me. *No, I don't want to!* An image flashes through my head—the image of me standing, leaning forward in the darkness at the top of the stairs in the town house. I remember how I wished I were far away, wished for the end. But I'm not done yet, not done keeping Mama company. I thought it was done, that the past was over, that I'd completed what needed to be finished, but I was wrong. There is more to do. There are things I need to say to other people, things I need to do for them. My sister, Peter, Leo . . . I squirm, make an effort to sit up, but fall back. I'm weak, but I want to live. I feel that with all my body now. Finally I manage to get some sound to come out of my throat.

"Please," I say, "don't kill me."

I make yet another attempt to stand up, supporting myself with my hand on the wooden deck, and this time I make it into a sitting position. Veronica backs away. Maybe she's preparing for another attack.

"Please," I beg. "Please don't kill me, please. I don't want to . . ."

I pull my shoulders up to my ears to protect my head and press one hand to my throbbing forehead. That's where the blood is coming from.

"What . . . what are you saying? Are you crazy?"

"I'm a friend," I continue. "I'm a neighbor. I know your son, Leo. He asked me . . ."

I look up to appeal to her sympathy. She's pressed against the door, with one hand on the handle as if she can't decide if she should stay out here or go in. Her face is completely pale, and she looks . . . wait now . . . She looks scared. Not enraged, not murderous, but scared—terrified, actually. But maybe I'm just imagining that. Maybe strong emotions all look similar. Maybe they contort facial expressions in a similar way? Veronica pushes down on the handle, and the door to the cabin slides open.

"Wait!" I yell. "Don't do it. Don't do anything you're going to regret."

But she goes in and closes the door behind her. The strength drains from me, and I fall back against the wooden deck, bloody and shivering. I roll to the side and listen, trying to hear what's going on inside the cabin. I can't hear a thing, no screaming, no banging. It's completely silent, almost as if Veronica is the only one in there, as if the cabin was empty when we got here.

I close my eyes and don't look up until I hear the door open again.

"You said you were . . . Who are you, actually?"

She twists the end of her high ponytail between her fingers, and her anxious eyes dart between me and the deck. When I follow her gaze, I see that the blood has trickled down and is smeared across the planks. It looks really macabre.

In a faint voice, I repeat what I said a few moments before. Veronica comes a little closer.

"Leo mentioned a neighbor who . . . Are you the author?"

I nod and wince. My forehead is burning and throbbing and there's blood everywhere.

"Please," I mumble again. "Don't hurt me. Don't kill me."

"Why do you keep saying that? Are you crazy?"

Her voice has gone up an octave.

"I called the police. They're on their way."

The police? *She* called the police?

"I want you to tell me why you're here now. Why did you follow me and try to jump me like some kind of freaking lunatic?"

For a few seconds there she seemed a bit calmer. Now she seems revved up again. Her eyes are wandering, and her voice is unsteady.

"Leo was worried," I manage to say. "I'm just trying to help out. I don't want you to do something you'll regret."

She shakes her head and makes a face as if what I'm saying is the strangest thing she's heard. I press my sleeve to my forehead, doing what I can to stanch the flow of blood. Even though I'm lying down, I feel dizzy.

"What happened?" I mumble.

"You're asking me what happened? *You* are asking *me* what happened? Oh, that's precious!"

She crosses her arms in front of her chest.

"I didn't notice you until I pulled onto the side road, but you must have been behind me for significantly longer than that, right? You scared me, do you get that? So much that I snuck out of the car and hid in the bushes. But you didn't drive by. You parked and . . ."

Her voice broke. Yet again, her eyes scan from the wooden deck beneath me to my face and then back to the bloody planks. One of my eyelids is starting to stick shut. If I'm not mistaken, the blood is starting to clot.

"It was just a push," she says. "But I guess it turned out to be pretty hard what with the adrenaline rush and everything. You fell and hit the railing, and I think . . . I think you have a gash over your eyebrow."

She's holding something in her hand. I see it gleam as she gesticulates. But it's not a knife. It's a key. That must have been what she was fumbling with, what she had dropped when we first confronted one another. Somehow I manage to raise myself into a sitting position. I don't dare stand up. I'm not sure my legs would hold me. Veronica doesn't take her eyes off me, and I see the faces she's making. The words she just said catch up to me, the frightened glint in her eyes as she described how she'd tried to hide from me, run away from me.

And suddenly it's just there, the realization that this whole thing was a mistake. Philip and the redhead aren't at the cabin. The reason the place looked so deserted, without any lights on, the reason I couldn't see any other car besides Veronica's outside is that no one else is here, only the two of us. My chest tightens, and the dizziness comes over me again.

"I'm sorry. I promised Leo that I would . . . but I . . . I should have known better."

I think I need to lie down again. I realize that I might faint otherwise, but I can't move. I press my sleeve to my forehead, trying to dab at my head with the parts of the fabric that aren't soaked through yet. I'm so cold now that I'm shivering.

Veronica is stamping her feet as she stands there.

"There's . . . We have a first-aid kit in the cabin. I could go get—"

"That's not necessary," I manage to say. "I think the bleeding is stopping."

She squints down at me.

"This business about Leo being worried. What do you mean by that? What is he worried about?"

"He mostly wanted to know that you were OK. And where you were going."

Her face stiffens.

"The plan was for his dad to tell him that we . . . that I was coming here. But apparently he didn't get the message. I did leave a note."

I nod cautiously, avoiding moving too much or too vigorously. I speak as slowly as I can, since my voice is distorted by my chattering teeth.

"Like I said, he just wanted someone to check on you and make sure you were OK."

Her face relaxes now.

"He has a good heart, my son."

Seconds tick by. The police should be here soon. I hope they have a warm blanket with them.

"You've seen each other a few times?"

I nod again. And then, as if to explain away or play down our interactions, I add that he evidently wants to become an author, too.

"Yeah," Veronica says. "So I understand. He has a very active imagination, Leo does. Too active for his own good sometimes."

She hesitates for a few seconds. Then she straightens her back and looks me straight in the eye.

"Come inside for a bit," she says in a tone that won't take no for an answer. "That wound needs to be cleaned. There's no way around it."

45

She stands beside me as I get up. She doesn't help me but seems ready to step in if I should fall. Then I shuffle into the cabin after her, step over the threshold straight into a large living room. It's dark and very cold. The way it is in a cabin where no one's turned on the heat, where no one's been for a long time. The realization hits me yet again: *No one is here.*

Veronica flips a switch, and the room is instantly bathed in light. She shows me the way to the bathroom and takes out the first-aid kit and a half-filled package of gauze.

"Here," she says, handing me some gauze. "I don't think you're going to need stitches. It doesn't look like it."

I lean over the sink and start cleaning my face. Veronica disappears but soon returns with a long-sleeved T-shirt and a fleece jacket as well as a bag for me to put my dirty clothes into.

"We must wear about the same size," she says, without making eye contact.

Then she closes the door and leaves me alone. I clean myself up in the sink, carefully washing around the gash on my forehead. It's swollen and tender, but I quickly determine that Veronica is probably right. The wound is wide but not particularly deep. And it's already started to clot over, as I'd thought. When I come back out, wearing her clothes and with a bandage on my forehead, she's sitting in an armchair in front of a coffee table with a glass of whiskey.

"There's something I don't understand," she says.

She shakes her glass gently in her hand, and the ice clinks. At first I felt OK, but now I notice how weak my legs are. The dizziness is lurking somewhere.

"You don't know me. At all. And yet you let yourself get caught up in Leo's anxiety, so much so that you drove out here. Can you explain why?"

Just then the room does a somersault before my eyes, and my field of vision flickers. I hear Veronica's voice more distantly now. It tells me to lie down on the sofa. She guides me there, and I sink into the cushions. I close my eyes for a long while, and when I look up again there's a glass of orange juice on my side of the table. Somehow I manage to lean forward, take a couple of sips, and then fall back onto the sofa again.

Veronica crosses one leg over the other and takes a drink of her whiskey. Now her face shows no sign of fear. Maybe because I'm so weak. Or because she knows the police will be here soon.

"Tell me. How did you end up becoming worried as well?"

My first thought is that I don't need to answer, that I don't owe her an explanation. Then I think about the drive out here and how I ran across the lawn after her, of the terror in her eyes when she turned around and realized I was right behind her. The moment when I realized that neither Philip nor the redhead were here.

I lean forward and drink a little more juice.

"It was . . . it was something I saw."

Veronica doesn't take her eyes off me. Close up like this, she's almost unimaginably beautiful.

"Something you saw?"

I open my mouth and hear myself telling her about that morning, what I witnessed from my kitchen, the flowers and the scissors, the hacking, chopping, and tearing, that tattered bouquet and the subsequent screaming and crying.

At first Veronica looks pale and then flushed.

"Oh, that," she says. "Yes, that was . . . I appreciate how that must have looked strange, strange and a little . . . crazy, maybe."

She raises her glass to her lips but immediately lowers it again.

"That wasn't like me at all, but there is an explanation, you know."

Then she tells me that she was supposed to go away that weekend. It had been planned for ages, and Philip had promised he would stay home with Leo. But the day she was supposed to leave, he told her that he had to go on a business trip, a meeting that had been set at the last minute, an important client that needed him.

"I objected, said that he knew how much I was looking forward to getting away. But he went anyway, even though he knew it meant that I'd be forced to cancel my plans. I was so incredibly angry. I guess I sort of lost control a little."

She brings the glass to her lips again, and this time she drinks most of its contents. I stare at the hollows in her neck, watch the skin moving as she swallows. It's as if something has been triggered within me, something I can't stop.

"Then, just two or three days after that, I saw something else, too. You were eating dinner. You started crying and ran out of the kitchen. After that you didn't come—"

Veronica sets her almost empty glass on the coffee table between us with a little bang.

"What is this, some kind of hobby of yours, sitting at your kitchen table and watching us? Is that what I'm meant to understand?"

I try not to tense up, try to sound honest and apologetic at the same time.

"It's happened. A couple of times."

"Why? Don't you have a life of your own?"

Her tone is sharp.

"No, I guess I don't. Not since my husband and I separated."

That stops her.

"Oh" is all she says.

My headache returns, and I close my eyes. Then I happen to think of my sister, who's still at my place, waiting. I have to get hold of her and tell her I'm OK. I feel my pockets but can't locate my phone. Then I remember the bag with my bloody clothes. My vest is in there, too. My phone must be in one of the pockets. I sit up and reach for the bag, then rummage around in it until I find what I'm looking for. I type a quick text to my sister and put the phone away. Surely I'm feeling a little better now that I've rested for a bit? If I just take something for my headache, I'll probably be able to drive home.

"I should, uh, I should probably be . . ."

Then I remember and carefully turn my head to peer out the window. The road through the woods out there is dark and empty.

"Shouldn't the police be here by now?"

But Veronica doesn't seem to hear me. She's busy refilling her whiskey glass.

"Can I ask why?" she says, putting the cork back into the bottle.

"Why what?"

"Why did you separate?"

I squirm.

"We're not divorced. It's a trial separation."

"A trial separation? What does that mean?"

"Well, the idea is for us to spend three months apart and then decide how to proceed, if we're going to proceed."

Veronica carefully taps her wedding ring against the glass in her hand.

"And?"

"I'm sorry?"

"What do you think will happen? Are you going to save the marriage or get divorced?"

Something flickers through me. *Please come home. I love you, always have, always will.*

"I don't know," I say, looking down.

Something in the bag by my feet beeps, and I realize that must be my sister responding to the text I just sent her. My temples are throbbing. I don't know what to do, don't know what's expected of me. I don't feel sure of anything anymore.

Veronica's voice reaches me, tears me away from my own thoughts.

". . . about my wanting to go back to school, that's why we're fighting, Philip and me. Because he can't get it into his head how important it is to me, that I'm being serious."

She cocks her head to the side.

"You know what I mean?"

I lean back on the sofa, then forward again.

"Yes . . . I . . . maybe."

Veronica takes another swig of the whiskey.

"You know," she says, "I left the university with only one year to go before I earned my degree."

She was pregnant with Leo and thought she could finish the last few classes after her maternity leave. But the years passed, and it never seemed to be the right time. It never worked, either because Leo was too little or—usually—because Philip's career wouldn't permit it. She took various part-time jobs and waited for it to be her turn.

"'Your turn will come, honey. Your turn will come.' It became a sort of mantra. I don't really know when he stopped repeating that— maybe when Leo was five or six. Something happened at that time. I think Philip sort of got used to having me stay home and started to really enjoy it. But by then, I wasn't doing very well at all. I'd lost all my energy and was . . . well, I simply wasn't a good mother. Thank goodness Leo was little. He doesn't remember very much from that age."

I ask if she has anything I can take for my headache, and Veronica brings me a pill and a glass of water. She's a good way through another glass of whiskey.

These days, she says, Philip sings a completely different tune. He encourages her to explore her creativity, find her own way of expressing herself. And god knows, she's tried. Watercolors, pencil drawing, silversmithing . . . you name it, she's tried it. But something has always gotten in the way. The paintbrushes broke, the tongs she was supposed to use for silversmithing disappeared.

"At first I didn't understand why, but then, well, it was obvious! It was never the intention for me to do any of those things. I don't need to explore my creativity. I need to finish my degree. I don't want a hobby—I want a job! I want to do the work I went to school for. There's nothing wrong with yoga, but if I need to listen to another 'om' during work hours, I'll—"

Veronica glances quickly in my direction. Her eyes have grown foggy, and she laughs, a hard, joyless sound.

"Maybe it'd be best if I didn't finish that thought."

She explains that she signed up for a low-residency distance-learning program, a way of getting going on her degree again. It was supposed to start with a weekend seminar with required attendance, but that was the weekend she wasn't able to get away. Now, she apparently has to wait at least a year for the next seminar to come along.

"The worst thing is that Philip doesn't understand how much that class meant to me. He can tell I was disappointed, but he thinks he can make it up to me by giving me things, as if I need more earrings or spa visits or surprise parties."

There's another ping from my bag. I hesitate, but Veronica is so involved in her account that it would seem impolite to pull out my phone. It's as if someone pushed a button and now she has to get everything she's been holding back off her chest, everything that has apparently built up over a number of years. If there's anyone who can understand what that feels like, it's me.

"Anyway. So he took me to this spa last weekend, and then I told him that I don't want any more lavish birthday presents, that what I need from him is something completely different. I really thought I'd gotten through to him, thought he had finally understood, but then I found out that he was planning a surprise party for me here at the cabin. One of our mutual acquaintances accidentally let the cat out of the bag. Philip had apparently asked her to help arrange all the practical details."

A mutual acquaintance. I picture Philip and the redhead: them disappearing into a building's front door, leaning over a restaurant table, making plans and chatting about the cabin. *A surprise party? How could I have been so wrong?*

Veronica has gotten up now and is pacing back and forth in the room.

"He was trying to be nice, he said, when I backed him up against the wall. But I don't get what he was thinking. I mean, given how badly I've been doing lately, how disappointed I've been in him . . . how could he think that the solution was a party? It wasn't until I said he should scrap the party that he understood how serious this was. Or maybe it was when I said I needed some space to think, that I wanted to come up here on my own for the weekend."

I empty the juice glass and then pull my hands inside the sleeves of the fleece jacket.

"Are you cold? The radiator should have started warming the place up by now."

I heave myself forward and sit on the very edge of the sofa.

"If you're planning to report me to the police for something . . ."

"Pfff," she says, reaching up to finger one of her earrings.

I look up at her questioningly.

"I didn't know if I should call the police or the ambulance. And then I realized who you are, that you're a neighbor, someone Leo knows. And I thought that . . . well, maybe we didn't need to involve the police after all. But all that blood on the deck . . . well, that would . . . maybe that would be hard to explain. And you're totally fine now, right?"

Our eyes meet. If I'm not mistaken, she looks like she's feeling a little guilty.

"So you . . . never called the police?"

She shakes her head.

"Leo likes you. True, I've been a little distracted lately, but I've gleaned that much, at any rate."

Leo. I screw up my eyes. There's something I'm looking for, the answer to a question that I'm not really sure how to ask.

"We've kind of neglected him a bit, both of us. Philip and I. He's always done such a good job of looking after himself. It's easy to forget that he . . ."

When I look up again, Veronica's eyes are trained on some invisible point in the distance. Then she blinks and sets down her glass.

"I'm going to deal with this," she says decisively. "I'll talk to him."

I think of the pen marks on Leo's neck, of his stolen shoes, and of all the other things. I carefully nod in response, say that that sounds good. Then I support myself with my hands and get up off the sofa. We stand facing each other for a few awkward seconds. Then Veronica reaches her hand out to me and I take it. She's as warm as I am cold.

"You'll get your clothes back as soon as I've washed them."

She says there's no hurry, that we're sure to run into each other again in the future. Otherwise, she knows where I live, she adds with a wry smile.

On the way to my car, I take out my phone. My sister has sent two texts. Great that you're OK, the first one reads. Let me know if anything comes up. PS: Respond with a NO if you DON'T want me to read your manuscript while you're gone. There's not much else to do here.

At first I think she's kidding, then I remember. Her reminder of how she used to read through my writing. That I once told her she had a flair for the dramatic arts. I hold my breath and bring up her second text.

No protest? I'll take that as a yes. I'm going to read it now. See you soon.

46

THE HUSBAND

My wife talks, and I listen. Her voice is calm, but it's clear from her face what a strain it is to revisit and talk about the events that followed her faked abortion.

The wound became infected and she developed a fever, but her mind was made up. Her former boyfriend would not get away with what he'd done. Even if it was the last thing she did, she would get even. She had settled on a night when her parents were going out to dinner. The fever was raging in her body. Her mother and father had no idea why, but they left her home alone with instructions to rest and drink plenty of fluids. As soon as they walked out the door, she got to work. She took the items she'd gathered out of the closet—rope, blindfold, duct tape, balaclava, knife, and hammer. She put everything into a small backpack and started to dress in dark clothing from head to toe. Pulling the pants on over the throbbing wound on her stomach was so painful that she saw stars, and yet she forced herself to continue.

It wasn't hard to figure out where her ex-boyfriend would be that night. At home with his new girlfriend, of course. She had been there several times before, snuck around the house and sat hidden behind a big boulder in the nearby wooded area. Sooner or later, he would come out the back where there was a flowerpot full of old cigarette butts. He would stand there for a while, and she could smell the smoke, see the little glowing point that was his cigarette through the dark. She never got any closer. He was always alone at those moments. The new girlfriend apparently didn't smoke but preferred to wait inside where it was warm, in front of the TV or maybe in the bed.

My wife says that she took her backpack and walked toward the front door. She was so dizzy that she had to support herself against the walls in the front hallway to remain upright. This night, she wasn't going to settle for watching from afar. This night she wouldn't watch while her ex disappeared back into the house and then just slink home filled with the same dark despair as when she had left. The plan was to step out of hiding and lure him into the woods, threaten him with the knife if she had to. Once in the cover of the trees and the darkness, she would put duct tape over his mouth and tie him up so he wouldn't be able to interrupt her or walk away. Then he would hear everything she had to say—*everything*. He would listen until he comprehended exactly how betrayed, degraded, and vulnerable his infidelity and subsequent ridicule had made her feel. He would beg for forgiveness. If he refused, there was always the hammer.

It wasn't a watertight plan. It had a lot of potential holes and shortcomings. She'd actually been planning to wait and prepare even more, but then she developed the infection and realized it was bad, that it was only a matter of time before she collapsed. She wasn't worried about her health. She was worried about the prospect of not being able to carry out her plan. She didn't care how it went, didn't care whether she dropped dead afterward, as long as she got back at him.

Tying her shoelaces took forever since it required bending over, a motion that made her scream in pain. When she finally straightened back up, her face pallid and her vision swimming, she did so just as the front door opened and her parents walked in. Evidently there'd been some misunderstanding. Their dinner party was actually the following weekend. They rolled their eyes and laughed at their own airheaded ways until it dawned on them what they were seeing before them.

My wife remembers only fragmentary images of what happened after that. She knows that she lunged for the door, and that her mother caught her and prevented her from leaving. She knows that someone screamed, and she understands that it was her. She knows that she screamed terrible things about her ex-boyfriend and what she wanted to do to him. She knows that she hit and kicked like crazy as they held her tight, restraining her. She knows that she hated her parents for not letting her go, for preventing her from carrying out her plan. And she remembers how her body finally collapsed, how she fell into her mother's arms and was embraced by her safety and love.

Up to this point, she hadn't allowed herself to cry. Not when she realized that her boyfriend was cheating on her with someone else, not when he dumped her, not when he trampled on her dignity. Not even when the sharp edge of the knife cut into her flesh. But the tears came at that moment, with her mother's arms around her and her mother's calming words in her ears: "This isn't what you want, this isn't who you are."

My wife pauses and looks down at her hands. I try to imagine the incomprehensible pain and desperation she must have felt, and I think that I ought to try to meet her partway. But I can't find the words. Instead I just wait mutely for her to continue.

Her parents must have discovered the wound on her belly, because they took her to the hospital right away. She doesn't remember telling them what she did to herself, but they found out somehow. They were both shocked, but her father took it the hardest. He apparently never got over it. After that he wouldn't look his daughter in the eye. Instead he would always direct his gaze at a point just above her shoulder.

Her mother was also heartsick. As parents, how could they have missed what was happening in their daughter's life? Certainly they had suspected that she wasn't doing well. For example, they had definitely noticed that she'd grown quite thin recently, but they'd somehow hoped it was a phase that would pass. What happened was like an alarm. During the first weeks, her mother didn't leave her daughter's side. She made sure that she ate. She slept beside her and stood constant vigil over her. Time passed, and slowly my wife came back to life. She started at the university, made new friends, and developed new hopes for the future. But it would take a long time before she dared to love again, and none of her romantic relationships lasted very long until she met me.

We look into each other's eyes.

"You are the first person I could imagine telling all this," my wife says.

"And yet you waited. You waited several years. You didn't say anything until after we were already married. And you didn't tell me the whole story until now."

She nods slowly.

"I wanted to tell you the truth, all of it, but every time I decided to give it a shot, I got scared, scared that you would look at me differently afterward, that you would stop loving me, and turn away. That you would . . . turn to someone else."

I avert my gaze, feeling my face grow hot. What my wife feared . . . had actually happened . . . Strangely enough, only now does the extent of my betrayal sink in. I betrayed my wife despite all she's been through, even though I knew that another man's infidelity in the past had almost destroyed her. How could this have happened?

Before I learned how my wife got the scar on her stomach, I had never even looked at another woman. I was so strongly and unwaveringly convinced that it would be the two of us forever. But the truth upended everything, made me view the woman I thought I knew so well in a different light. Something stole in between us, and I let it happen. I betrayed her, disappointed her, and lied to her. But have I stopped loving her? No, I don't think I have.

I'm about to move forward and take her into my arms, but then I picture her eyes the way they just looked. I remember how black they became, how I had the sense that she was going to shove me over the edge. I think about Anna's worry and discomfort, about the questions she asked me about my wife when we last spoke on the phone. *Has she shown any other signs of violence or a desire for revenge?* The doubt has returned, and instead of pulling closer to her, I lean back a bit.

"What you did to yourself then, what you were prepared to do to your ex-boyfriend—how do I know that that's not how you still are, deep down inside?"

She doesn't answer right away, and when she eventually does, her voice is quiet, scarcely audible.

"There were times when I myself was unsure. Now I know, without a doubt, that what my mother said was true. That's not what I want, not who I am. But only you can say how *you* feel about that."

Seconds turn to minutes as we sit there in silence. I know what she's waiting for, but I can't give it to her. I just can't, not right now, not yet. Finally I look up and into her eyes again.

"I don't know what I want. I need more time."

I'm prepared for these words to cause her to break down and start crying. Or return to the bedroom and descend again into her passive state. But nothing like that happens. Instead she nods and clasps her hands in her lap.

"All right, then."

Then she says that she thinks we should separate, that she loves me, but that she can't do this anymore—that it's better that we each reflect and decide what we want as individuals and how we will proceed together.

Separate? She can't be serious, can she? But yes, I can tell from her face that she is. Suddenly it feels as if all the oxygen has gone out of the room. Perhaps I'm unsure what I need and want, but I know one thing: Loneliness isn't it.

My wife straightens up.

"I hope you'll decide that you can love all of me, who I once was and who I am, without fear and without disgust."

Then she gets her suitcase.

Then she starts packing.

Then she's gone.

47

ELENA

It's really late by the time I park my sister's car on the street outside the yard. It's Friday night, and I meet a group of dressed-up happy young people moving down the sidewalk. The group parts to let me through. I feel like a shadowy figure as I pass them, a dark spot in the middle of all that glitz and merriment.

The light is on in the Storms' kitchen, and I see two people sitting across from each other at the table in there: Philip and Leo. I wonder what they're talking about, wonder if Veronica's precipitous departure forced a new and different type of conversation between father and son, one that will lead to something good.

I sent Leo a text before I left the cabin.

Your mom is OK. She'll be in touch with you.

The response came right away.

I know. I'm talking to her right now.

I turn toward my house across from theirs, the one I will soon have spent half of my planned time in. Unlike the Storms' home, none of the lights are on. My sister is somewhere in there, waiting. Maybe she fell asleep, although I doubt it. I haven't called. I made do with texting her before I left Veronica. I wrote that I was on my way but didn't respond to her question about reading the manuscript. Opening the front door, I wonder if she's really read it. At any rate, I'll tell her everything now, everything. I kick off my shoes, hang up my jacket, and call out hello. I don't get an answer.

She's sitting in the dark in the kitchen, in the same seat where I myself have spent so many hours. I didn't see her from outside, but she must have seen me through the window. The stack of papers I printed out earlier today is sitting on the table in front of her. Even without any lights on, she notices my borrowed clothes and the bandage on my forehead and asks how I am, but her voice is somewhere else, lost in other thoughts.

I cautiously set the car key down on the counter. I don't need to wonder anymore if she's read it. Or if she understands the nature of what I've written.

"How far did you manage to read before you . . . understood?"

"Before I realized that the story was about you and Peter?"

I nod.

"Maybe the part about the . . . scar."

I tense up and want to bring my hand to my abdomen. My fingertips twitch, but I resist the old, ingrained impulse. I don't need to hide anymore. The truth is free. I have set it free.

"Although I had been told it was from an appendectomy. The barbed-wire-fence-when-you-were-a-kid explanation wouldn't have worked on me."

No, it wouldn't have. My sister and I know all about each other's childhoods, every accident, every scrape. That's how close we were back then.

"Thomas," she says now, "your first boyfriend. I hardly remember him. I think I only met him a couple of times."

I shift my weight from foot to foot as she mentions his name.

"We were going to move in together. We had just decided that."

My sister slowly shakes her head.

"I never had any idea that your relationship was so serious. I guess I thought it was one of those teenage things that would pass."

She had lived abroad for so many years, moving back and forth between various places. It's not so strange that she doesn't remember every single detail in the life of her little sister, who's six years younger. But it's time for me to correct her about this specific part.

"I was a teenager when we started dating, but I was twenty-one when it ended."

My sister's eyes gleam. She is quiet for a while.

"And that thing Mama told me," she said then, "about the anorexia. How does that fit into all this?"

I lean back against the counter.

"I stopped eating when I found out that Thomas was seeing someone else behind my back. More as a reflex than a conscious choice. I just didn't have any appetite anymore. I lost a fair amount of weight, but it wasn't anorexia. After what happened . . . after what I did and what I could have done. It was such a terrible disgrace in Mama's eyes. She could say anything, just not the truth."

My sister turns to the window. Perhaps we're thinking about the same thing. Of the secret Mama had kept. And of what she chose to say instead. Perhaps my sister is also wondering why.

"You didn't want her to tell the truth, not even to me."

"Especially not to you."

I wonder if my sister detests me now. Will she distance herself from me, just when we were starting to become close again?

"I mean, just look at how things turned out with Papa," I add.

She turns on the kitchen chair, wondering what I mean. I explain that the relationship between Papa and me was never the same after that night when he and Mama came home earlier than expected and caught me in the front hall, sick and thirsty for revenge. Sure, he was present and involved in the beginning. He must have been. But then, once I recovered and returned to living, he pulled away, and I noticed that he had a hard time looking me in the eye. I don't know if he was feeling fear or revulsion, and I don't know if it was mostly the self-harm or the thought of what I was capable of doing to Thomas. I just know that the distance between us grew and grew.

"It was my fault, that he left so suddenly after Mama's death, that he moved so far away. I've always known that, always felt guilty that your relationship with him also ran out into the sand. I was the one he was trying to get away from, but it was as if you—"

"Elena, you're not responsible for an idiot acting like an idiot."

The words push their way up, sticking in my throat.

"I'm sorry." *For what I did. For lying to you all these years.*

Then she gets up and comes over to me, comes closer and closer until she's standing right in front of me.

"It must have been so incredibly awful for you. I can hardly imagine it. I'm sure no one can. And when I think of everything you've been through . . . Without my having any clue, without my being able to be there for you."

She wraps both arms around me and holds me, hugs me tight.

"That's over now. From now on, you're not alone anymore. Never again, for as long as I live."

My emotions are all in a jumble inside me. My longing to sink into my sister's embrace—to lean into her and release my tears—is strong, but something else is stronger. I carefully free myself from her hug.

"That's not all," I say. "I've done something else, something even more awful. If you've read the whole text, from beginning to end, then you know what kind of a person I am."

"What I know," my sister says resolutely, "is that you're my sister. We'll deal with one thing at a time, and right now you need to eat. Eating disorder or not, you're skinny as a string bean, and it's not healthy, Elena. People need to eat. Otherwise they die."

She pushes me down onto a chair and takes some food out of the fridge, explains that she went shopping while I was out. There are cold cuts, several different types of cheese and olives, crackers and grapes. She evidently also picked up a bottle of wine. She must have gone shopping before she read my story, when she still thought we'd have a relatively normal Friday night once I returned. Now everything is all upside down. We both know that, but my sister is still soldiering on. She strikes a match, touching it to the wicks of a few tea lights and setting them on the table between us.

I look askance at her as she sets out plates and glasses. What is going on inside her? What does she think about everything she's just read? She must have a thousand questions.

"I was about to tell Peter," I mumble. "Right when Leo came over."

My sister slices a few pieces of cheese and places them, along with a little ham and a couple of crackers, on a plate that she pushes over to me.

"You said that he'd been in touch, and something about an accident."

She stuffs an olive into her mouth and then prepares a plate for herself. I stare at the food in front of me.

"To begin with . . . we tried to get pregnant. Yes, that was it. And we tried for a long time, but we didn't decide to separate because of the infertility. You understand that now, right?"

She nods slightly and pours wine into my glass. I'm not planning to drink any of it, not until I've gotten everything off my chest that needs to be said. Somehow, I need to get through the painful chain of events that occurred after Peter admitted his infidelity to me. I need to explain how it felt to learn that he had been inside another woman, not just once but multiple times. I need to express what it felt like to realize that he wasn't planning to ask for forgiveness, that he didn't even know if he wanted our relationship to continue or not. I need to express how this pulled the rug out from under my feet and how I—for the second time in my life—totally lost both my stability and my footing.

I need to tell about the days I spent in bed, how night and day blended together until the black gradually had streaks of red in it. The fantasies about blood and revenge. The speculative book I bought, the shady internet searches, the secret jogs, my surreptitious weight lifting, the muscles I tensed to the breaking point, the fantasies that grew increasingly violent, that felt more and more real. I needed to tell my sister about all of it. My throat grows dry and rough, and my eyes wander over to the stack of pages that is lying on the counter now. *Or maybe I don't need to describe anything at all. Maybe that's exactly what I've already done.*

"Simply put, I wanted to kill him," I say hoarsely. "I felt more and more like I could really do it."

I finger the base of the wineglass.

"And this time, Mama wasn't by my side."

No Mama to put her arms around me, hold me, help me hold on. No Mama who wouldn't lose faith in me, who would continue to love me no matter what.

My sister takes another olive. I wish we didn't have to go through all this, but there's no other way around things that are painful. Not if we're going to find our way back to a relationship built on genuine communication and intimacy.

"Earlier today you were talking about what it was like before Peter and I separated. You said you could tell that something wasn't right between us, that when you called and asked, I changed the topic and started talking about something else. It's true, but that renovation in the stairs, it was . . . it was maybe more important than it seemed."

She pulls an olive pit out of her mouth and sets it on the edge of her plate.

"I'm listening," she says.

Then I tell her about the elevator. Because of the building renovation, the elevator was temporarily out of order, but the engineering inspection would later show that there was something loose in the elevator doors up at the top, on the eighteenth floor, our floor. When Peter went to work the next morning, he happened to forget all the notices about the elevator being out of order, and he pressed the button out of habit. The door slid open, and he stepped forward. He didn't notice until he was already standing on the edge that the only thing underneath his feet was an empty elevator shaft.

The room remains silent for a few seconds. Then my sister stands up and walks over to the counter to retrieve the stack of printed pages. She flips through them until she finds what she's looking for. Then she reads aloud.

"I'm teetering on the edge. I turn around and our eyes meet, hers the same ones that once looked into mine at the altar in that picturesque little village church. They were filled with tears and emotion then, but now they're black with the hatred of revenge. This whole time I've been worried about her . . . Suddenly I realize that I should have been afraid for myself."

She raises a quizzical eyebrow, as if to check whether she's at the right place in the text. I nod, and she leans over the table. The glow of the tea lights flickers over her cheeks.

"So what actually happened?"

I turn to look at the neat row of olive pits on her plate.

What happened was that I stood inside the door to our apartment and observed Peter through the keyhole, just as I did every morning. He didn't know I was standing there, couldn't feel my eyes on him, but as soon as he walked out our door, I staggered over to it. Every time he left, I wondered if he was really going to work or if he was actually on his way to meet *her*. My eyes were glued to his back. I could never tear myself away from the keyhole until I had seen him step into the elevator and go on his way. But on this specific morning, something else happened.

"I saw the elevator doors open, saw Peter take a step forward and then freeze, midmotion. That same instant, I happened to think of the renovation and remembered that the elevator was going to be out of order. The next instant, I'd flung open the door and was heading toward him. It all happened so fast . . ."

I stop. The silence grows between us. Finally my sister picks up the stack of pages again and continues reading aloud. Maybe she thinks it's easier this way. Maybe the text provides some sort of distance to what we're talking about, even if it's all my words.

"Everything happens so quickly, and yet the moment stretches out and lasts for an eternity. She comes closer, is right up next to me. She raises one hand, then the other. Soon I'll fall. Soon I'll be dashed to pieces. Soon it will be over. Three, two, one. Now."

She looks up.

"So Peter thought you were willing to murder him to get revenge, that you rushed out into the stairwell to push him into the elevator shaft?"

The edges of the Brie have softened, and the wine remains untouched, even in my sister's glass. I force myself to look her straight in the eye.

"What do *you* think? What do you think I was planning to do?"

My sister sets down the stack of printed pages and looks away for a fraction of a second. Then she looks up and, in a steady voice, says: "I know you, Elena. You would never kill anyone."

My sister puts her hand over mine and squeezes it cautiously. I stare at her fingers.

"No," I say, "I wouldn't."

There are so many things I'm not sure about. I don't know what would have happened if my mother and father hadn't come home early that night fifteen years ago. I don't know if my sick body would have carried me all the way to Thomas's new girlfriend's house or whether I'd have been able to put my plan into action. I'll never know if, when it really mattered, I would have been capable of using the knife and the hammer for anything other than threats. Nor can I fathom how it was possible for me to cut and stitch up my own flesh—that the thought ever occurred to me, that I managed to do it without fainting from the pain.

Then there are the things I *am* sure about. I know that what I did to myself was something gruesome, verging on barbaric, and I will always live with the white marks on my skin that serve as a reminder. After Peter admitted to cheating on me, I fantasized about injuring or even killing him, and I know that those fantasies took an increasingly realistic and frightening form. But I also know that when I saw him by the elevator doors that morning, helpless and vulnerable on the edge of a precipice, there was only one thought in my mind: I needed to save him. The look in Peter's eyes as I rushed toward him, on the other hand, revealed that he believed something totally different.

My sister pushes away the wineglasses and pours us water. I bring the glass to my lips and drink several gulps.

"So this whole text, that you wrote it at all, is this some kind of . . . I mean, is this an attempt to . . ."

My sister's hand rotates in the air, seeking, searching. I turn to the window and look out across the yard. The light is off in the kitchen opposite us now. Leo and his father are no longer visible.

"I started writing because I saw some things, the kind of things that reminded me of what Peter and I had been through. At first I wasn't really going anywhere with the text. They were just words that came to me that wanted out. But then . . . then it turned into something else."

My sister checks to see what I'm looking at, and I realize that all my ramblings about the neighbors are fresh in her mind. She raises her hand and cautiously touches the bandage on my forehead, finally asks what happened, where I went tonight. But I can't get into that now. My bewilderment, confusing my own life with what was going on in the house opposite me . . . I can't explain that. I don't really even understand it myself, not yet. I need time to let the whole situation settle, let all the parts fall into place.

"When Peter got in touch with me," I continue instead, "I realized that he wanted to get back together. That's when the text became something different. I thought that if I wrote down what happened, if I did that as ruthlessly and honestly as possible, maybe that could be a way of understanding and forgiving Peter. But most of all, of understanding and forgiving myself. That's the only way we could have any chance of continuing our relationship."

My sister picks up my plate and holds it out to me. I stuff a little strip of prosciutto into my mouth. The hunger is there somewhere, but I can't taste the food.

"Mama always said that work was the best medicine. You said the same thing, not too long ago."

She takes a bite of cracker.

"Yeah, I haven't forgotten. Plus that writing advice I reminded you about—to dig where you stand."

"That's literally what I did this time."

We sit in silence for a while before I go on.

"Ever since Mama died, I've been afraid something would happen, that I would wind up in some extreme situation of some kind. I've been worried about how I'd react if that happened. I've worried that maybe I would lose it again, not be able to rely on myself. Then this stuff with Peter happened, and I wavered, definitely, but when it came down to it, I did nothing . . . nothing that Mama wouldn't have been proud of."

I poke at one of the tea lights and watch its flame flicker.

"It was such a relief, the awareness that I would never again do anything like what I had done, what I was about to do when I was young. That I was able to cope, thanks to Mama, but also that I could cope without her."

My sister has taken my hand in hers, and she's carefully stroking it. I shiver. A black shadow hangs over the kitchen table.

"But what happened afterward . . ."

My voice fails me, and I cautiously pull my hand back, take hold of my water glass again and empty it.

There was someplace she needed to go. There was someone she needed to visit. After that everything would be over. Order would be restored. The filth that had been would be erased once and for all.

My sister's hand is still resting on the table, but I pretend not to see it, can't permit myself any signs of affection as I describe what happened afterward, as I describe the day I went to see Anna.

48

THE HUSBAND

Someone calls me. I don't know who. A girlfriend—that's how she introduces herself. She's not crying, not to begin with, but her voice is muted. She says Anna's name and asks if we were very close. I'm completely at a loss for what to say.

"I'm sorry?"

"Your number is in her contacts list on her phone, so I'm just wondering how you knew each other."

There's no suspicion or insinuation in her voice. Even so, I'm flummoxed. Eventually I manage to say that we've met each other a few times through work. Then it hits me.

Were very close. *Knew.* Why is she using the past tense?

"We're helping contact all her acquaintances," the woman continues. "Her family asked us to do that."

I freeze.

"There was an accident. It happened quickly. They say she probably didn't suffer."

She says that she's a friend of Anna's from her book club. They were supposed to get together that night, and it was Anna's turn to host. But when the first women arrived at her place, they realized right away that something was wrong. The door was unlocked, and the fire alarm was going off inside. The charred remnants of the pie Anna was presumably planning to serve were in the oven. The table hadn't been set yet. Apparently she hadn't gotten to that. There was no way to be sure of what she'd gone down to the basement to get. Napkins, maybe, or even more likely, a couple of bottles of wine.

They found her at the bottom of the basement stairs, a steep, precipitous, treacherous fall. She was lying on the floor with one leg at an unnatural angle, her eyes staring blankly. One of the women screamed. Another had the presence of mind to call for an ambulance. When the EMTs arrived, they determined that Anna had broken her neck, probably in a couple of places and probably as the result of an accident, a "slip and fall." She was wearing high-heeled shoes. She really loved heels. And apparently she'd gone up and down those stairs many times before, but it's so easy for an accident to happen.

"A terrible, tragic accident, as I said."

By this point, the woman on the other end of the line is quietly crying, the woman who had been tasked with calling to notify me. Then she pulls herself together and blows her nose. She says nothing can bring Anna back to life, but that it's important to the family for everyone who knew her to be notified as soon as possible.

"We've all gathered over here now, those of us who were closest to her, at her place with her family. We think this is what she would have wanted."

I mumble in agreement, and she wishes me well. I thank her, and we hang up. Afterward I sit for a long time with the phone in my hand, staring into space. *When did I last see Anna? Or talk to her on the phone?* Actually maybe it wasn't that long ago, but it still feels that way. It feels like an eternity.

The distance between us grew quickly after we lay there in the bed and Anna said that stuff about my wife: *She doesn't seem normal.* Afterward, I realized that something important happened at that moment, that it was as if an invisible force changed directions then and there, from having brought us closer to each other the whole time to now starting to pull us apart. What once appeared unabashedly obvious between us vanished and was replaced by Anna's discomfort and anxious thoughts.

I started letting more time go by between phone calls. I canceled a date we had planned and then another one. Anna didn't object, so I assumed we both felt the same way. We had filled some kind of emptiness in each other's lives for a while, and now that was over. Our relationship was fading away on its own. That's what I thought, but that's not what happened. The end came in a completely different way, quickly and decisively.

A terrible, tragic accident.

I get up from the armchair on wobbly legs. The silence bounces between the walls while I survey what should have felt safe and familiar but didn't at all. At one time, not very long ago, I viewed this as a home. Since the separation, it's been reduced to a residence.

We've all gathered over here now, those of us who were closest to her, at her place with her family.

Anna had her family and her friends, people I don't know, women and men I've never met. When they got together after her death, no one asked about me. And that was as it should have been.

I walk over to the window and peer out. I'm struck by an acute desire to call my wife, while at the same time realizing that this is out of the question. We weren't supposed to have any contact at all for three months. That was our agreement, and I can't break our silence for this, just to tell her that the woman I cheated on her with is dead.

The only thing that would give me the right to get in touch is if I've made a decision about how I want to proceed, by getting divorced or staying together as a couple. I close my eyes. *When will I know?* Then I look up again.

Maybe deep down inside I actually already do know?

49

ELENA

I didn't want to know anything about her, the other woman. I made that very clear to Peter, several times.

And yet I couldn't help it. I had to find out who she was. With the help of his phone history and a few keystrokes on the computer, I learned her name and where she lived. When I decided to separate from Peter, I knew I wouldn't be able to move forward without talking to Anna. I needed to ask her some questions and assess the look on her face when she talked about him. This way, I convinced myself, I would find out if there was any chance of our marriage having a future.

I took the bus to her neighborhood at a time when I figured she'd probably be home from work. I hadn't called in advance. No one knew where I was or what I was planning to do. She lived in a small single-story house, and when I knocked on the front door, she was standing in the kitchen. I could see her through the window. She appeared to be checking on something in the oven. She had her frizzy hair down and was wearing an apron over her turquoise dress. She turned around and caught me looking in her window. She was beautiful. She looked puzzled when she opened the door, wondering if I was a friend of someone in the book club and perhaps they'd invited me. It wasn't until after she'd let me in and shut the door that I managed to identify myself.

She'd already started walking back to the kitchen, but when I told her my name, she spun around, teetering on her high heels. Once she turned back around to face me, I clearly could see that she wasn't just surprised, but rather afraid, terrified. What had Peter told her, actually? What had he said about me? I stepped closer to her.

"I kind of need to talk to you," I said, trying to sound as calm as possible. "Do you think we could sit down for a moment?"

Anna's eyes roved around the room, over my shoulder and back again. It seemed like she was looking for someone or something. Then I realized it was an expression of the discomfort she was feeling because I was between her and the door. She didn't believe what I'd said about talking. She thought I was planning to hurt her.

I took another couple of steps forward and said, "I just—"

I didn't get any further before she lunged for an open door somewhere between us. I hadn't thought of this before now, but Anna disappeared through that doorway and tried to slam it shut behind her, presumably in an attempt to stop me from following her. Instead, she must have tripped, because I heard a terrible crash, a piercing scream, and a few heavy thuds. Then it was completely silent.

I stood there frozen at first, then crept closer to the doorway. Cool air rushed up at me along a steep, narrow set of stairs down into the basement. Anna was lying on the floor at the bottom of the stairs, and as soon as I saw her, I knew she was dead. Even so, I called her name several times. When she didn't respond, I went down to her and put two fingers on her neck. There was no pulse beating under her skin anymore. Then I panicked. I raced back out the same way I'd come in, left the house and the neighborhood as fast as I could. The scope of what had happened didn't seriously sink in until later. *Dead.* Anna was dead because of me. True, I had no intention of harming her, but the fact remained: If I hadn't shown up unannounced on her doorstep, this irreversible event wouldn't have happened.

My sister sits quietly as I say all this. At some point, she gets up to put away the leftover food. Then she sits back down across from me and keeps listening. Of course she's aware of most of this from the last section of my manuscript. Still, I have the sense that it's only just now becoming real to her. When I'm done, I cast a quick glance at her serious face. I can see the little muscles beneath one of her eyes, twitching.

"I can't comprehend it," I say, resting my head in my hands. "I can't wrap my head around the fact that she's dead and I'm . . . that I was the one who . . ."

My voice breaks. I wait for my sister to say something else, anything at all, but she's quiet for a long time.

"So awful," she finally says. "Really awful."

Another few minutes pass in silence. Then my sister shivers, as if she's trying to clear all the images out of her mind. She looks up and our eyes meet.

"It wasn't your fault, Elena."

"I went into her home," I say roughly. "Something about the way I looked or the way I was acting frightened her. When I realized she was dead, I didn't call for help. I didn't notify the police or call an ambulance. I hightailed it out of there."

My sister doesn't respond right away, and I look off, staring at one of the tea-light flames until my field of vision warps and fills with strange colors.

For several days, I'd waited for the police to come storming in at any moment. I was sure they would have formed suspicions and detected evidence or fingerprints, or that someone in the neighborhood had seen a strange woman running from the house. But nothing happened. Then I saw the death announcement in the newspaper, and it said that Anna had been torn away from friends and family, shockingly and tragically. Nothing in the short obituary even hinted that there was anyone to blame for what happened. To the contrary. Days turned into weeks without anything happening. And then Peter got in touch.

"It wasn't your fault," my sister repeats. "You had a shock and you . . . But it wasn't your fault. It was an accident. Peter said the same thing, didn't he? Of all people, he certainly ought to know."

I blink. His words are still ringing in my ears: *She died, Elena. She's dead. That's what's happened. It was an accident, a sheer accident.*

The truth is that it wasn't up to me, my sister, or Peter to decide whether it was my mistake or not, my fault or not. But I don't say that out loud.

Not long after that, we call it a night. We're both exhausted, but my sister insists on spending the night, offering to sleep on the floor next to my bed. I protest weakly, saying that I'm used to being alone and that she doesn't need to stay for my sake. She strokes my cheek.

"Did you hear what I said before? From now on, you don't need to be alone anymore."

While I'm in the bathroom brushing my teeth, I hear her through the wall, talking to Walter and saying that she won't be home until the morning. Her voice is mild, and before they hang up, I hear her say, "I love you, too." Apparently love that lasts does exist; long-term relationships can work. It's nice to know. When I got it into my head that something wasn't right between my sister and her husband, I was probably just projecting my own experiences, just like with Philip and Veronica. I see that now.

I set down my toothbrush and look at myself in the bathroom mirror. Even though I see the part I played in what happened, some pieces of the story are still missing. There is only one person who can help me put them into place. I'll talk to him tomorrow.

50

When my sister wakes me, it's already late morning.

"I have to go," she says. "I have an appointment for a massage with a ruthless physical therapist. I would cancel it, but it would be hell trying to get a new appointment and . . ."

I wave her on her way. Of course she should go. I can handle things.

"But I'll call you afterward, OK?"

Even though I nod, she doesn't budge. I thwack her with my pillow. "Get going, then."

"Hey, sleepyhead," she laughs, heading for the door.

I throw the pillow after her but miss. She sticks her tongue out at me before disappearing down the stairs and, a few minutes later, out the front door. I stretch and realize that I'd slept straight through the whole night for the first time in a long time.

When I make it down to the kitchen, I see that my sister made a pot of tea. I drink a cup and eat some leftovers while I run through what the day might hold in store for me.

At regular intervals, I glance out the window. On one of those occasions, Leo is suddenly just there in the yard. He's sitting on that blue bench in front of the rhododendron bushes, not doing anything. From what I can see, he doesn't even have a book with him. He's just sitting there and drawing patterns on the ground with the tips of his shoes, as if he's waiting for someone.

A while later, I step out the door and walk over there.

"Can I have a seat?"

He nods and scoots over to make room.

"How's it going?" I ask.

He says that things are OK and gestures toward my forehead.

"What happened to you?"

I shrug and sit down beside him. The morning sun is shining right on us, and my cheeks feel warm. A minute or maybe two pass.

"Leo," I say then. "There are a few things I'd like to ask you about. Your mom and I talked for a long time yesterday when we got to the cabin and—"

"I was worried about her. For real! I actually was."

His voice breaks, and I lightly brush his one knee with my hand.

"No one thinks otherwise, Leo."

I turn my face to him, but he is still staring straight ahead.

"I want you to know that I didn't pass on any of what you told me. Neither about her nor—"

"That stuff about the purse," Leo interrupts heatedly, turning to face me. "That actually happened. She threw it in the water, on purpose. Maybe she thinks I was too little—that I don't remember. But I do. And she *has* been acting super weird lately."

I nod.

"OK. I have a feeling that she's going to want to talk all that over with you when she comes home. We'll make sure that happens, pure and simple. You shouldn't need to go around worrying about your parents. You're going to have your hands full being . . ."

I furrow my brow.

"How old are you, anyway?"

"Almost fourteen."

"OK. You're going to have your hands full being a hip cat."

One corner of his mouth curls into a smile, almost unnoticeably.

"Ha! I made you smile."

I give him a playful shove, and he shoves me back.

"No one says 'hip cat' anymore. No one under the age of fifty anyway."

Then he grows serious again.

"So what exactly did you guys talk about? You and my mom."

"Well, about you, about the benefits of having an active imagination among other things."

Leo blushes. Then it comes out. OK, maybe he did exaggerate a little bit, make insinuations, and fictionalize certain events. Like that stuff about the book *Getting Away with Murder*. He'd only seen that at my place, not at home.

"I really want to understand," I say. "How did it even occur to you to come up with something like that?"

Leo brushes his bangs off his face.

"I thought you would think it was exciting—more exciting than real life."

"And why was that important? What does it matter what I think?"

"Well, hello! Don't you get anything?"

We stare at each other for a few seconds. Then Leo says that he saw me even on my first day, the day my sister helped me move in. He recognized me but hardly dared to believe it was true. A real, live author on the same street, in the house right across from his!

He decided to meet me somehow and try to get to know me, but it took several weeks before he finally got up the courage to ring the doorbell. By then he'd found the interview where I described how I got my ideas and explained that my writing was often based on observations of the people around me.

Leo stops talking and gives me a knowing look.

"Do you mean . . . ," I begin. But I lose my train of thought and have to start over.

"Do you mean that you exaggerated and made up things about your mother because you . . . because you thought I would use it as material in a book?"

Leo chews on his lip.

"It seemed like it was working. Every time I said something about her, that she wasn't doing well or was a little crazy, I noticed that you listened extra closely."

On a visceral level, I object. *That isn't true,* I want to say. But then the moments flicker through my memory, one after another. Questions I asked, hints I dug more deeply into, moments when I allowed myself to be caught up in it all. Boundaries I transgressed with respect to both Leo and his parents.

And yet I'm the one sitting here asking for explanations. My shoulders droop. The conversation should have started from a completely different end.

"Sorry," I say. "I never meant to make you feel that way. I suppose you can say that I have my own demons. And I've done a lot of stupid things lately. None of that is your fault."

Leo leans forward, propping both elbows on his knees.

"Do you understand?" I continue cautiously, eager to really get through to him. "This whole thing is entirely my responsibility. I shouldn't have—"

Before I have a chance to finish my sentence, he tosses his head so his bangs fly to the side.

"Whatever. It's chill."

We sit there in silence for a bit. I think about the friend he told me about, the boy who moved a few months ago. Then I think about his situation at school. And about his feeling neglected, which I'd discovered by reading between the lines whenever his parents came up.

"Everyone needs someone to talk to," I say, "someone who cares. And I care about you, Leo, I do—for real."

In the bushes behind us, some magpies screech. One of them flutters away across the yard, seeming to have been thoroughly roughed up by the others.

"I want things to go well for you. No one has the right to treat you badly—no one."

He leans back again, says that some of the ninth-grade girls actually stepped up to defend him at the start of the week. They told off a couple of boys who had tripped him in the cafeteria and made them, if not exactly apologize, at least back down. Since then things have been a little better. He hopes this will continue.

"I hope so, too," I say. "Otherwise, you should let me know. Then maybe I'll write some of them into my next book as victims of a particularly brutal accident."

Leo shakes his head and laughs.

"You're a little nuts, you know."

Before I realize what's going on, he gives me a quick hug. My chest feels warm, and there's a prickling feeling in my eyes.

We sit for a while and chat before I finally get up and explain that I have to go. When Leo wonders where I'm headed, I say that I have an errand that can't wait. A cloud has covered the sun, so I zip up my vest.

"Oh, and," I add, "I don't think I ever said this, but your essay was really well written and moving. I hope you get a good grade on it."

Leo peers up at me from under his bangs.

"Oh, uh . . . that wasn't a school assignment. That was . . . my way of getting you to read something I wrote."

I stuff my hands into my pockets.

"OK. Well, anyway, it was a good story."

"It wasn't true."

"That's what's great about being an author. You don't always have to stick to the truth. It's actually better *not* to."

51

THE HUSBAND

Days pass and turn into weeks. One day when the weather is nice, I take a long walk. I pass an elderly couple slowly walking along, hand in hand. Their delicate fingers hold each other, and it's so obvious that they belong together—that they've been together for a long time and that they will remain that way until the end. As I pass, the man turns his watery light-blue eyes in my direction and smiles gently.

I have the sense that he's trying to communicate that life is fragile, that you need to hold on tight to what you love. It's far too easy to lose each other. I smile back. Sometimes, I think, you lose yourself.

At the park, I sit down on a bench to rest. I have a view of a little girl on a swing, hear her yelling to her dad and asking to be pushed faster. "Higher, higher," she yells, and when she turns her face in my direction, it startles me. Because the little girl's coloring is so much like my wife's; so are her almond-shaped eyes and just the same little dimple in each cheek when she laughs. The likeness is striking. It hits me: *She could have been our daughter.* And then: *What are we doing? What have we done?* The last remnants of uncertainty disappear. What had been foggy and dubious no longer is. Everything is so clear, clearer than it has ever been. I quickly get to my feet.

On my way home, there's something different about my steps, something purposeful. We were only supposed to be in touch if something happened, if one of us made a decision. But something actually *has* happened, something that made me see the world in a new light. I really want to explain this to my wife. If she would just consider meeting me, I'll tell her what I'm thinking, what I want.

And then? Then we'll see.

52

ELENA

I'm standing outside the police station. Soon I'll go inside and ask to speak to the officer on duty or whoever can take my account of what happened that afternoon at Anna's house. Then the question of my potential guilt can finally be resolved. Regardless of what happens, regardless of the outcome, I won't regret it. This is the only way forward, the only way for me to be able to live with myself in the future. I cast a quick glance up at the sky. *You would have come with me, I know.*

There's only one thing that remains to be done before I walk up the stairs to the front door. I pull out my phone and call a very familiar number. An instant later, he's there again, right up against my ear. My husband, my beloved.

"I've been thinking," I say, "about that stuff about getting together, you and me."

I don't get any further than that before Peter gives a yell. Eagerly he wonders if my call means that I'm done with whatever needed finishing up. I say yes.

"You can come home, you know, Elena. Any night at all works. I'll make us dinner—lamb and au gratin potatoes, your favorite."

He sounds so happy, and of course that makes everything much more difficult. At the same time, I can't help but wonder if I'm really the one he's been missing. Or if it's mostly the loneliness that makes him want us to get back together. I'll never know, and I suppose it doesn't matter.

I clear my throat.

"The reason I'm calling is to say that . . . well, that it's not a good idea for us to see each other."

At first he's confused. He thought that . . . he thought it sounded like . . . Then he pulls himself together and changes tack. If I need more time, that's totally fine. He's prepared to wait however long it takes if I'll only—

"No," I say. "You don't need to do that. I don't want you to do that."

Peter sounds even more flummoxed. I close my eyes, needing to get this over with as quickly as possible. Dragging this out just makes it more painful.

"This is the hardest thing I've done in my whole life, but I'm planning to file for divorce."

At first there's complete silence on the other end of the line. Then Peter finds his voice again.

"I'm sorry," he says. "I'm sorry for what I put you through, for betraying you and cheating on you. I don't think I said that clearly enough at the time, and I . . . well, I should have said it a long time ago."

I open my eyes again. It's as if I had been waiting to hear him say those words. At one time, it had burned inside me to demand them of him. Just as I'd wanted to demand them of Thomas fifteen years ago. My throat feels tight.

"Peter, I—"

"It was never about her," he continues quickly, "but rather about what happened between us, between you and me. Or, actually, I suppose it was mostly about me. That I didn't know how to handle what you told me. But now . . . I know that I can . . ."

He keeps talking, says things that lead my thoughts to a future I had previously hoped for and believed was possible. Now I know better, but it doesn't stop it from hurting inside. *If only everything had been different.*

"Peter," I interrupt softly. "I've made up my mind. There's no other way forward from here. I realize that now. I'm sorry."

I hear him breathing on the other end of the line, and there's so much more I want to say, so much I could say. I squeeze my hand around my phone and press my lips together. *Be strong. You need to be strong.*

"But why?" he wonders. "Don't you love me anymore?"

I take a deep breath. How can I explain? Where should I start?

"Lamb and au gratin potatoes was never my favorite meal, I think. It was yours. But since you were so fond of it, it had to become my favorite meal, too. Your love, our life together, meant everything to me. I had never had a successful relationship before, had never met anyone I loved so ardently and unconditionally, so I was desperately keen on making it work with you. I didn't know how to do that, just knew that more than anything else I wanted us to be compatible. I wanted you to feel that we were.

"So I made lamb and au gratin potatoes for you on special occasions and sometimes just on ordinary days, as well. I made it that night when you'd agreed to sit down and eat together and really talk. That night when I got dressed up and used the best china, when I hoped that we would find our way back to each other after the distance that had grown since I revealed my secret to you. That was the night you told me about Anna.

"I had brought home flowers. Perhaps you remember the bouquet that was on the kitchen table, or maybe you don't. When my tears and your attempts to comfort me ended, we went to bed and fell asleep from exhaustion. That's what you think, right? You don't know that I lay awake tossing and turning, that I finally got up and wandered around the apartment, hounded by something wild inside me. The flowers were still sitting in the vase in the kitchen, and when I saw them, something came over me, something I couldn't explain. Or didn't *want* to explain. That's when I got out the scissors.

"My scream didn't wake you up. At least, you didn't get up to see what was going on. And I didn't leave any traces. The only difference the next morning was that the flowers were gone. You never commented, so I assume you didn't notice they were gone. Maybe, as I said, you hadn't noticed they were there, either. Maybe you only noticed half of my efforts for that dinner, that night. Maybe it was like that the whole time we were together."

"Really? Have you stopped loving me, Elena?"

No, I could say, *I haven't—not yet—not by a long shot.* I bite my lip and can't help but think of the voicemail he left me the other day. *I love you, always have, always will.* But words are one thing, and actions are another. I wait until I'm sure that I can keep my voice steady.

"Thanks," I say then. "Even though it ended badly, I want to thank you for these years, for showing me the joy of being close to another person. I will take that with me, the knowledge that it's possible, that it's worth it."

The words sound overbearing, but that can't be helped. They need to be said. I need to say them.

"So this is really over, Elena? Do you mean that?"

This won't be the last time we talk to each other, I realize. We're going to need to deal with all the practical matters—sign the paperwork and divvy up our things. But we'll say goodbye now. I feel that clearly, here and now.

"Goodbye, Peter. Promise you'll take care of yourself."

We hang up, and I almost succeed in holding back my tears. When I look up the staircase at the police station's front door, both the view and my vision are foggy. But my resolve doesn't waver when it comes to this, either. Slowly I begin to walk up there, one step at a time.

53

It's Sunday afternoon, and despite the tentative sunshine peeking over the roofs, the yard is empty. Veronica came home a few hours ago. I saw her open the trunk of her SUV and unload her suitcases onto the sidewalk. Philip came out to meet her and gave her a long hug before they carried the things into the house and closed the front door behind them. Since then there's been no sighting of anyone from the Storm family.

I drum my fingers on the edge of the table and look down at the paper in front of me. The plan was for me to write a shopping list, but at the same time there are so many other things swimming around in my head.

I wonder how Leo is doing and how he's feeling. And then of course I think about what happened at the police station yesterday. I was shown into an office where I spoke to a man in a uniform with a receding hairline. He had friendly eyes. I thought that several times during our conversation. He took notes while I talked and asked a few clarifying questions, but mostly he listened. He said they'd be in touch with me soon and then told me I was free to go.

"It was good that you came in," he said.

Just what exactly those words meant remains to be seen. I'm prepared to accept the consequences of my actions, no matter what they are. A possible prison sentence doesn't frighten me. For the first time in a long time, I feel something resembling faith in the future, even hope. What I've been through, what I'm still going through, is a tunnel, not a dead end.

I bring the pen to the paper. My sister is coming over for dinner tomorrow even though it's a totally normal weekday. She pretty much invited herself, and I said she could come on one condition: that she brings Walter. I remember how affectionate and warm her voice was when I heard them talking on the phone through the bathroom wall. If she and I are going to strengthen our relationship, it makes sense for Walter to be a part of that, too. Besides, I need more people in my life, not fewer. In reality, it's kind of lame for a puzzle to only have two pieces.

The only question is what kind of food to make. Anything besides lasagna, I think, and catch myself sniggering a little at my sister's lack of culinary imagination. Once I've jotted down the ingredients for a curry recipe that doesn't seem too hard to make, I add a few other things to my list, the kinds of things I may need for the week ahead. Fruits and vegetables, whole-grain bread and rice, turkey and salmon fillet. I should start eating properly again, taking care of myself. *You need to eat . . . otherwise you'll die,* as my sister had said last Friday night. And I don't want to die, not yet.

Mama. My pen stops. How long does it take for frozen grief to melt away once it's begun to thaw? There's no definitive answer to this question, but at least I'm not alone anymore. My sister and I can help each other handle the longing when it strikes or when something new pops up that Mama turns out to have said or done, the kind of thing we maybe don't always understand. I twirl the pen in my hand and shake my head. That thing my sister told me, what my mother had told her about me . . . I still can't get it to add up.

I can't decide if it's a blow to the image of my mother or if it simply adds some nuance. Maybe I don't need to decide. Maybe it's enough to point out that she wasn't superhuman, that like any other person, she must have struggled with doubt and anguish—and no one wants anything other than to do right by their child, even at times when that's damned near impossible.

The doorbell surprises me. *Leo!* I look up and peer out the window. But the person standing outside and raising her hand when our eyes meet through the glass isn't Leo.

"Hi," Veronica says when I open the door. "Am I disturbing you?"

Her long honey-colored hair is pulled back as usual, although there's something different about her. Maybe the fact that she's not wearing any makeup at all. I shake my head. No, she's not disturbing me.

"I don't really know what I'm doing here, but . . ."

We eye each other for a brief moment.

"Or, well, I do know of course. I wanted to ask how you're doing."

My hand flies up to my forehead automatically. The cut still burns and feels tight, but it's healing. The scar will scarcely be noticeable.

"Plus," Veronica continues, "I kind of wanted to try to explain myself a little. I feel like I sort of went on and on up there at the cabin, talked as if there was no tomorrow."

She hesitantly tugs on the collar of her sweater, says that she read somewhere that something dramatic can have that effect, that shock and adrenaline can make people open up to total strangers and say things they never would have said otherwise.

"I was really shaken. One minute I was being pursued by a crazy person, the next minute you were lying on our deck in a pool of blood and raving about how I shouldn't kill you."

She quickly makes a face.

"And then there was the alcohol on top of that."

I clear my throat and pull my cardigan together over my chest.

"I . . . It did all get a little fraught, all of it."

"I think you could safely say that."

She laughs, and in her laugh I hear the echo of Leo's. Otherwise there's not much resemblance, at least not in their appearance.

"At any rate," she continues, "I think we're going to solve this. Philip was really excited when I came home. Said that only now did he understand how preoccupied he's been with his own affairs, that for a long time he hadn't really been noticing me or Leo properly and that he was ashamed of it. He even cried, and it seemed as if—"

Veronica stops.

"There I go, going on and on again," she says rolling her eyes at herself. "Oversharing."

"Don't worry about it."

She flashes me a quick smile.

"Maybe it wasn't just the shock and the whiskey, after all. Maybe there's something about you, too, something that makes people . . . well, that it's easy to say too much to you, extremely easy. Could it be that whole author thing? That you're one of those people who sees things? And listens, maybe? That's what Leo says, that you're a good listener."

"How's he doing?" I ask.

Veronica scratches her arm, says that the two of them sat down and talked for a long time today as well. It wasn't an easy conversation, but for the first time in ages, she felt like they'd actually managed to get through to each other.

"As I said, he thinks very highly of you. 'More grown-ups should be like her.' I'm pretty sure that's what he said when you came up."

"If only more teenagers were like him," I respond.

Veronica laughs again, and a strange sensation comes over me. A feeling that there's something that unites us, her and me, something that can't be seen from the outside. Of course it could be even bigger, bigger than both of us. Maybe more women than you would think have hacked apart bouquets of roses in a fit of rage. Maybe more ought to.

Veronica checks the clock and says she's got to be getting back home. Then she looks up again and our eyes meet.

"I hope things work out for you and your husband, too," she adds. "Or at least for you."

Yet again, I hear Peter's words ringing in my ears. *Don't you love me anymore? Have you stopped loving me, Elena?* Maybe he didn't understand that the question was phrased wrong. It wasn't *my* love that fell short, it was *his*.

I tell Veronica to say hi to Leo, and we say goodbye. After I close the door behind her, I slowly roam into the living room and over to the bookshelf. I run my hand over the spines of the books and feel the force of all the stories hiding within flow into my body.

Early tomorrow I'll call the agency and ask for some new editing projects. Or maybe not. Maybe I should take a walk instead and visit a café downtown, or simply sit down at the kitchen table and see what turns up outside my window.

I'm not the same woman as before, nor am I the author I once was. If and when I start writing something new, I'm going to keep an eye on myself, be very attentive to the sometimes-thin, but crucial, dividing line between reality and fiction, be careful not to confuse myself with other people. But, that said, I'm still an observer, and I know that good stories are everywhere, sometimes where you suspect them least of all. All you have to do is keep your eyes open.

ACKNOWLEDGMENTS

THANK YOU.

Among authors, you sometimes hear talk of the "difficult second book." Well, I'd like to introduce a new concept: the difficult *fourth* book.

Compared with my first three books, the process of writing this one felt longer and bumpier. On the other hand, memory can play tricks on you, so maybe (as my husband claims) I'm tossed back and forth like this between hope and despair every time. Maybe that's part of being an author. At any rate, that certainly makes the support and encouragement I receive from the people around me all the more precious.

Thanks to Bokförlaget Forum, with publisher Adam Dahlin and editor Kerstin Ödeen at the helm, for believing in me and always pushing me to write the best book I can write. Thanks as well to the rest of the gang at Bonnier in sales, marketing, PR, etc., and who have been working hard to get my books out to readers around the country.

I also want to avail myself of this opportunity to thank all the booksellers from north to south. Some of you are very near to my heart. I hope and trust that you know who you are—no one mentioned, no one forgotten.

Since the previous book, *The Missing*, my stories are also reaching readers beyond Sweden. This is thanks to Elisabet Brännström and Amanda Bértolo Alderin at Bonnier Rights—who, as I write this, have sold the rights to a dizzying twenty-six countries. You've also been stable sounding boards during the writing process itself. My warmest thanks for that.

In connection with this, I also want to be sure to thank my foreign publishers for their confidence and for their single-minded efforts in building my authorship in their respective markets.

With gratitude to my translator, Tara F. Chace, and to the entire team at AmazonCrossing, for being supportive and professional through every step of the process.

I am both humbled and amazed to see not one but two of my books now having been translated into English, thus making it possible for me to reach readers across the world.

A very special thank you to my editor, Elizabeth DeNoma, without whose trust, passion, and insistent work this would still be but a dream.

Thank you to my test readers, Maria, Sofia, Alexandra, and Louise, for taking your work seriously, giving your time, and providing constructive feedback.

A special thank-you to all the wonderful readers and listeners (especially podcast listeners!) for the energy and encouragement you provide.

Thank you also to my family, relatives, and wonderful friends inside and outside the world of writing.

Mom and Dad, thank you for your general verve and devotion, and for your wise opinions and warm hugs that one afternoon in March in particular.

Johanna, for our conversation, which means so much to me.

Ninni, for being there to celebrate with me when things are going well and (when necessary) to help me pick up the pieces when they're not. For being my own little treasure—friend, colleague, and mentor all in one.

Niklas, for making me believe I could finish writing this book, even when I doubted it. Especially then. To you, Max and Molly: In the end, everything is about you. Thank you for being in my life. I love you.

Caroline
Täby, Sweden, June 2017

ABOUT THE AUTHOR

Photo © 2015

Caroline Eriksson holds a master's degree in social psychology and worked for more than ten years in human-resource management before deciding to pursue writing, her childhood dream. Her first two novels are based on historical Swedish murder cases, and her debut, *The Devil Helped Me*, was nominated for *Stora Ljudbokspriset* (the Big Audiobook Prize) in 2014.

Caroline has lived all over the world. She attended high school in Quantico, Virginia; studied at the University of Adelaide in Australia; and now lives in Stockholm. She denies being a daredevil but admits that she once threw herself off a mountain in New Zealand in a hang-gliding experiment.

Her greatest adventure today is raising her two children, and she satisfies any residual wanderlust by exploring the most terrifying parts of life—its dark psychological elements—in her writing. *The Watcher* is Caroline's second psychological suspense thriller and her second book translated into English.

ABOUT THE TRANSLATOR

Photo © 2006 Libby Lewis

Tara F. Chace has translated more than twenty-five novels from Norwegian, Swedish, and Danish. She earned her PhD in Scandinavian languages and literature from the University of Washington and lives in Seattle with her family.